Beast Mode

Yuvaraj

Disclaimer

The events and characters depicted in this book are fictional. Any resemblance to actual persons, living or dead, or actual events is purely coincidental.

The narrative includes high-stakes action, intense violence, and adrenaline-pumping sequences intended for entertainment purposes. Reader discretion is advised.

The author does not endorse or encourage any dangerous behaviours or actions depicted in this book.

Dear Reader,

First of all, thank you for picking up this book. This action story began as an idea in mid-2020. Over time, I worked on it whenever I could. Initially, I had hoped to turn it into a film, but in 2024, while working at a bookstore, many customers asked me for recommendations for short action books. This inspired me to adapt my story into a novella.

If you're looking for a quick action-packed read, I hope you enjoy this book.

Thanks again,

Yuvaraj

Prelude

Arjun eased the motorcycle forward, its engine humming softly in the oppressive stillness. The road ahead glistened faintly under the pale, uneven glow of the streetlights. Something lay sprawled on the asphalt—a motionless shape that caught his attention. His knuckles whitened on the handlebars, and his eyes flicked between the parked cars and shadowed windows lining the street.

He shut off the engine and swung his leg over the motorcycle, his boots scraping lightly against the pavement. The sound, though soft, seemed to reverberate in the empty night, setting his teeth on edge. The shape didn't stir. His pulse thundered as he approached, each hesitant step tightening his shoulders with anticipation. He flexed his fingers, barely aware of the tension that curled them into fists.

"Hey," he called, his voice low and sharp, slicing through the stillness.

The shape jerked upright with terrifying speed. A hand—no, a vise of iron—clamped around his throat. Arjun's breath vanished in an instant, his vision narrowing to the pale, featureless face of his attacker. He staggered back, boots skidding on the asphalt, his hands clawing instinctively at the crushing grip. His lungs burned, his chest convulsing for air as he shoved against the man's chest.

With a gasp, he broke free, stumbling as the world spun.

Relief was fleeting.

A fist crashed into his jaw, whipping his head sideways. Fire erupted along his nerves, but instinct took over. He blocked the next strike, his forearm stinging from the impact, and drove his fist into the man's ribs. A grunt escaped his attacker as he staggered back, and Arjun seized the opening, throwing a kick that landed solidly in the man's midsection. The attacker crumpled to the ground.

Before Arjun could catch his breath, another shadow loomed behind him.

Rough hands clamped onto his arms, yanking them back. He thrashed against the hold, adrenaline surging, but the first man was already rising. Their blows came hard and fast, each one tearing another shard of strength from him. Pain blurred into a relentless rhythm, and his legs buckled, dropping him hard onto the pavement.

Through the haze of agony, he caught the flash of movement as one of them mounted his motorcycle. The familiar growl of the engine turned foreign, cruel. The second man stood over him, his presence a lead weight in the dark. They moved without urgency, knowing he couldn't stop them. The motorcycle roared as it disappeared into the night, its taillight shrinking to a distant ember before vanishing entirely.

Arjun lay there, his breath hitching in ragged bursts. The asphalt pressed cold against his cheek, dampened by the faint scent of oil and lingering rain. His fingers twitched, curling into a weak fist as the dull ache in his knuckles punctuated the sharper fire in his ribs.

He stared after the stolen motorcycle, the void it left behind swallowing the night in deafening silence.

Rage simmered beneath his exhaustion, as sharp and real as the pain—a promise of what was yet to come.

1

The bat rested lightly against Rahul's shoulder as he surveyed the road ahead—cracked and pockmarked, but theirs for now. Traffic buzzed faintly in the background, a distant symphony beneath the sharp laughter and shouts of his friends. The chalk lines of their makeshift pitch stretched across the asphalt, uneven but defiant, a claim staked in the face of a city that barely noticed them.

Sanjay's arm whipped forward, and the ball sailed in a spinning arc, a fleeting blur against the sky. Rahul stepped in, muscles coiling, the bat meeting the ball with a sharp, clean crack. It shot past a parked cab, vanishing into the shadows of the alley beyond.

"Four!" Rahul bellowed, his voice cutting through the air. His friends erupted, their cheers bouncing between the buildings. The thrill surged through him—unstoppable, electric.

Then came the creak.

The cab door opened. A slow, deliberate sound that sliced through their excitement like a blade.

Rahul's stomach tightened. His fingers twitched against the bat's worn handle.

Rajeev stepped out, the weight of him enough to still the street. His father's presence always carried a gravity that threatened to pull everything down with it. Dark eyes swept over the pitch, taking in the chalk lines, the defiance, the sheer audacity of it all. Then, they landed on Rahul.

"Rahul." The name came like a whip crack, sharp and unforgiving.

Silence. The laughter was gone. The world shrank to just the two of them.

Rahul swallowed, but the dryness in his throat remained. "What, Dad?"

Rajeev took a step forward, the city's noise retreating behind him. "Out here again? After everything I've told you?" His voice was low—like a slow-burning fuse. "Skipped lunch again, too? Anyway, you should be at home. Studying."

Rahul felt the bat grow heavier in his grip. He tightened his fingers around it as if bracing himself. "I'll eat after the match dad" he said, forcing a smirk. "Don't embarrass me—my friends are watching."

Rajeev's jaw tensed, his gaze unwavering. The space between them became a battlefield, neither willing to be the first to step back.

A car horn blared in the distance. A moment passed. Then another.

Finally, his father exhaled, shaking his head—something unreadable flickering across his face. Disappointment? Resignation?

"We'll talk at home," Rajeev said, voice steady but final.

The cab door slammed shut, its echo hanging in the air long after he was gone.

Rahul turned back to his friends, throwing on a grin that didn't quite reach his eyes. But the spark had faded, the match now just another game, the thrill replaced by something heavier. Something he couldn't quite shake.

2

Rajeev handed Meera the groceries without a word. The kitchen smelled faintly of turmeric and soap, a scent that usually wrapped the space in warmth. But today, it did little to soften the tightness in his chest.

"He's out there again," Rajeev muttered, leaning heavily against the counter. His voice carried the weight of something older than this moment. "Careless. No discipline."

Meera, steady at the cutting board, didn't look up. "At least he's outside," she said, her tone light but pointed. "Better than being glued to that phone."

Rajeev exhaled sharply, a bitter chuckle escaping before he could stop it. "You always do this," he said, shaking his head. "You make excuses. The phone, the motorcycle, every time he throws a tantrum, you just—"

Meera's knife hesitated against the wood. "And if I hadn't?" she asked, her voice quiet, measured. "Would you have handled it any better?"

Rajeev scoffed, the sound dry, but there was something else beneath it. "Don't get me started on his hair," he added, almost as if needing to redirect. "Growing it out like girls now. What's next? Braids? Hair clips?" His hands gestured vaguely, his irritation searching for an outlet. "And you encourage it, don't you?"

Meera's lips twitched, a small, reluctant amusement flickering there. "Hair clips would be practical, at least," she mused, eyes still on the vegetables. "Keep it out of his eyes."

Rajeev stared at her, momentarily disarmed. "This isn't funny, Meera."

"No," she agreed, finally setting the knife down. "It's tragic. The boy's hair is clearly a national crisis."

Something between them shifted, unspoken but heavy. Rajeev's frustration cracked just enough to let something older slip through—resentment, exhaustion, regret. "He manipulates us," he said, softer now. "And we cave. And now look—he doesn't care about anything but himself."

Meera met his gaze, and for a long moment, she said nothing. Not because she had nothing to say, but because there was too much. The silence stretched, weighty, familiar. Then she turned back to her work, the steady rhythm of chopping filling the space between them.

Rajeev swallowed, grabbed his keys from the hook by the door, and stepped outside. Sliding into the cab, his fingers curled around the wheel. For a moment, he just sat there, staring at his buzzing phone, its screen lighting up the quiet night—a familiar lifeline.

A new request—Road No. 12.

Without hesitation, Rajeev accepted. The engine rumbled to life as he pulled away, his house shrinking in the rearview mirror.

3

Rajeev drove to the pickup point and slowed as he approached the location, tapping the brakes out of habit. The cab shuddered violently, the tires skidding slightly before it groaned to a halt. He gripped the wheel tighter, his pulse quickening. "Damn it," he muttered. He had been meaning to get the brakes checked for weeks. Now was not the time for them to fail him. He exhaled, shaking his head as he leaned back in his seat, trying to ignore the growing unease creeping up his spine.

A man jogged up to the cab, his breath ragged, his face slick with sweat. His shirt was torn, a dark smear staining the fabric near his ribs. He yanked open the door and threw himself inside, slamming it shut with a force that made Rajeev flinch.

"7186. That's the OTP," the man said, his voice low but urgent. He barely paused before adding, "Now drive!"

Rajeev turned in his seat, frowning. "You alright, sir?"

"Yes, yes, just go!" Anwar snapped, his hands gripping the edge of the seat like he was bracing for impact. His eyes flicked to the rearview mirror, wild and desperate.

Rajeev adjusted it—and his stomach clenched. Three men were sprinting toward the cab, their silhouettes cutting sharply against the dim streetlights. One of them reached into his jacket.

"Shit," Rajeev breathed. Instinct took over. He slammed his foot on the accelerator, the engine roaring in protest before the cab lurched forward. Tires screeched against the asphalt, and the figures in the mirror grew smaller—but their fury was unmistakable. The cab swerved as he pushed it harder, the city blurring past.

4

Rajeev's arms ached from gripping the wheel too tightly—this chase had gone on longer than he could handle.

Rajeev gripped the steering wheel, the leather slick against his sweaty palms. The cab hurtled through the city's narrow lanes, buildings blurring into streaks of gray and beige. In the backseat, Anwar ducked low, his head jerking up every few seconds to peer out of the rear window, now shattered into a spiderweb of cracks.

The motorcycles' engines roared, the sound clawing at Rajeev's ears and spurring his foot harder onto the pedal.

"They're still coming!" Anwar's voice cracked, the fear in it pressing against the already claustrophobic air in the cab.

Rajeev's throat tightened. "Who are these people? What did you do?" His words were clipped, anger and panic warring for dominance. His eyes flicked to the rearview mirror, catching the glint of helmets bearing down on them.

"Just drive, man! I'll explain later!" Anwar's reply was a desperate plea, his body coiled like a spring against the seat.

Rajeev's jaw clenched as he swerved sharply, narrowly missing a fruit cart. Bananas tumbled onto the street, their bright yellow skins sliding under the tires of an oncoming rickshaw. A shout erupted behind them, fading as Rajeev's cab careened forward.

"Watch it!" Anwar yelped, clutching the seat as the cab jolted over a pothole. Rajeev ignored him, his eyes darting between the road and the shadowed figures of the motorcyclers gaining ground.

One rider sped up, his gloved fist pounding against the window. The sound reverberated through the cab, sending a jolt of adrenaline through Rajeev. He yanked the wheel left, the cab lurching violently and forcing the motorcycle to veer away.

"Goddamn lunatics," Rajeev muttered, though his voice trembled. His gaze darted forward, catching the flash of two more motorcycles blocking the narrow lane ahead. His breath hitched.

"They're cutting us off!" Anwar's words came fast, a tremor weaving through them.

Rajeev slammed on the brakes, the tires screeching in protest as he threw the cab into reverse. His pulse pounded in his ears, drowning out Anwar's panicked muttering. The motorcyclers closed in, their silhouettes distorted in the cab's cracked side mirror.

A crash shook the vehicle as one rider leapt onto the hood, his boots thudding against the metal. Rajeev's breath caught, his hands freezing on the wheel for a heartbeat too long.

"Move!" Anwar's shout snapped him out of it.

Rajeev twisted the wheel violently, the motion throwing the rider off balance. He hit the pavement with a sickening thud, rolling to the side as the cab shot forward. Anwar exhaled shakily beside him.

But the relief was fleeting. The brakes groaned under Rajeev's foot, but the car didn't slow. He slammed the pedal again, his mind reeling. "No, no—brakes are gone!"

"What do you mean gone?" Anwar's voice pitched higher, panic spilling into the cab.

The pole loomed ahead, its metal frame glaring in the midday sun. Rajeev twisted the wheel desperately, but the steering locked. His heart felt like it stopped even before the crash.

The cab crumpled on impact, the front collapsing like a tin can. Steam hissed from under the mangled hood, mixing with the acrid stench of burnt rubber. The silence that followed was deafening, broken only by the faint hum of motorcycles idling a few meters away.

The crowd thickened around them almost immediately. Curious faces pressed closer, voices rising in a chaotic chorus of questions and shouts. A few brave onlookers stepped forward, pulling the cab doors open to help Rajeev and Anwar out.

The motorcyclers, realizing the growing mob, exchanged glances before revving their engines and retreating into the labyrinth of streets.

5

The sound of the crowd still echoed faintly in Rajeev's mind as he lay in the hospital bed, his leg encased in stiff gauze. He didn't remember much after the crash—only the blur of strangers pulling him from the cab and the shrill wail of an ambulance. Now, the sterile smell of antiseptic replaced the acrid stench of burnt rubber, and the hum of the hospital drowned out the chaos of the streets.

The door burst open, pulling him from his thoughts. Rahul rushed in, his face pale, his steps quick and purposeful. Behind him, Meera followed, her voice tremulous as she tried to keep up. "Rahul, slow down!" Her voice trembled as she called after him, "Rahul, slow down!"

Rahul ignored her, his heart pounding in a way that made his breaths short and uneven. He pushed open the door to the small hospital room. Inside, Rajeev sat on the hospital bed, his left hand wrapped in a bandage and his right leg stiff, covered completely in white gauze. He looked worn out but upright, his face calm, as though forcing himself to seem fine.

"Dad…" Rahul breathed, his eyes darting from the bandages to his father's tired face. The sight struck him harder than he expected. His dad had always seemed indestructible, always quick to correct or criticize, never slowing down—until now.

Rajeev glanced up, managing a small smile.

Meera entered behind Rahul, wiping her tears with the end of her saree. Rahul barely registered her presence. His focus stayed on his dad.

"What happened?" Rahul asked, his voice tense, almost demanding.

Rajeev sighed, glancing down at his bandaged hand. "Nothing much. A few scratches here and there. That's all."

Rahul frowned, his frustration bubbling to the surface. "Scratches? Dad, you're sitting here with half your leg bandaged. Stop pretending it's nothing."

Rajeev's voice softened, tinged with weariness. "Just leave it, Rahul. Nothing happened to me, but the cab… it's damaged. Repairs will take time. Insurance money… Well, that'll come when it does. And—" He hesitated, rubbing the back of his neck. "All our savings… they're gone. The hospital bills…"

Rahul's jaw tightened. He stepped closer, his voice steady but firm. "Come on, Dad. Nothing major happened. We'll manage. I'll figure it out."

Rajeev looked up at him, his tired eyes reflecting something unspoken. Rahul felt a pang of guilt and something more—a resolve he hadn't experienced before.

The door creaked open. Anwar stepped inside, his face pale, his right hand also bandaged. He looked down, clearly uneasy. "Sir.. I—I'm sorry. Because of me..."

Rajeev raised his hand lightly, cutting him off. "It's done now. Forget it."

Anwar hesitated. "I... If there's anything—"

"Nothing," Rajeev's voice was firm, yet polite. "You can leave now. Be careful, okay?"

Anwar looked at Rahul, then back at Rajeev, guilt written all over his face. With a small nod, he turned and quietly left the room.

Rahul watched him go, his jaw tightening. He looked at his father's bandaged leg and then at the closed door, his fists curling at his sides. The memory of the crash and the hospital bills burned in his mind. "He's the reason all this happened," he said, his voice low but sharp. "You could've asked him for money, Dad."

Rajeev shook his head immediately. "No, Rahul. He looks like he's dealing with dangerous people. Better to stay away."

"Dangerous? What do you mean?"

Rajeev didn't answer directly. He glanced at Meera, then back at Rahul. "Just listen to me. Stay away from him."

Rahul didn't argue further, but his expression stayed hard. His gaze lingered on his father's bandaged leg, his breath hitching slightly. The sight made him think of all the times his father had seemed invincible, and now, here he was—wounded and vulnerable. He turned to look out of the small hospital window, his hands gripping the sill tightly as a heaviness settled in his chest. Turning to look out of the small hospital window, he felt something shift within him—an unfamiliar sense of responsibility.

The room settled into silence, except for the faint sounds of the hospital corridor outside.

6

The chai shop bustled with noise, a blend of clinking glasses, sizzling kettles, and animated chatter. The air was thick with the scent of cardamom and boiling tea leaves, wrapping itself around Rahul like a memory he couldn't shake. He leaned back on the bench, his arms crossed, a faint smirk tugging at the corner of his lips, but his eyes—those betrayed the storm raging inside him.

Across from him, Sanjay sipped his chai, watching him with mild curiosity.

"I still can't believe Dad didn't ask Anwar for money," Rahul muttered, shaking his head. His voice was low but edged with frustration. "I mean, the guy literally walked in there looking guilty as hell. If he caused the accident, he should've helped pay. It's only fair."

Sanjay raised a brow. "Your dad's a proud man, bro. He doesn't want to owe anyone."

Rahul exhaled sharply, his smirk vanishing. He stared into his chai, fingers drumming against the table in an erratic rhythm. "Yeah, well, good for me." His tone carried a sharp edge of sarcasm, but he avoided Sanjay's gaze. The tightness in his shoulders, the way his jaw clenched—everything about him bristled with unspoken frustration. "Now I get to step in and be the hero. Maybe Dad will finally stop talking to me like I'm some reckless guy who can't handle responsibility."

Sanjay leaned forward, elbows on the table. His gaze flicked to Rahul's motorcycle parked outside, gleaming under the dim streetlights. "You know, you've got that motorcycle sitting there. My cousin started a food delivery job last month. Says it's not bad if you don't mind the grind."

Rahul blinked, considering it. "Food delivery?"

Sanjay shrugged. "Why not? You have a motorcycle. Just download the app and start earning. It's quick money. I'll get my cousin's referral code so both of you can get the joining and referral bonus."

Rahul's fingers tightened around his cup. His father's bandaged hands, the slow way he had walked into the house after the accident, flashed before his eyes. The anger, the helplessness—they tangled in his chest, forming something new. Something sharper. This wasn't just about proving himself anymore. This was about stepping up. About survival.

He tapped the edge of the table, the chai shop's noise fading into the background. His pulse thrummed in his ears as the weight of the decision settled on his shoulders.

He nodded, slower this time. "Alright. I'll do it." His voice had lost its sarcasm. Now, it was firm, certain. "Instead of wasting time looking for another job, this is the better option—plus, I'll be my own boss."

Rahul leaned back and let out a slow breath, his gaze fixed on nothing in particular.

A week later

7

Rahul straddled his motorcycle, staring blankly at the delivery app on his phone. The midday sun hung heavy, its heat wrapping around him like a suffocating blanket. Sweat pooled at the base of his neck, but he ignored it. There was no time to complain.

Life had turned into a blur of deliveries—one stop after another.

In the mornings, he squeezed through narrow lanes, maneuvering past parked cars and speeding autos, balancing the food bags on one hand while dodging potholes. At noon, the air burned like fire, and he'd find himself stuck at red lights that seemed to last forever, the smell of exhaust and fried food mixing in the hot wind.

"Where are you? You're late!" The voice on the other end of the phone snapped, cutting through the hum of the city.

By afternoon, every stop began to feel the same: impatient customers snatching orders without so much as a thank you, doors slamming before he could utter a word.

"Can't you deliver faster?" someone grumbled one day.

"Next time, don't take so much time!" said another, tapping his watch.

Each small insult chipped away at him. He would clench his jaw, swallow the retort that burned on his tongue, and ride on. He'd learned to tune out the sharp edges of their words, focusing instead on the steady vibration of his motorcycle beneath him.

Evenings brought traffic jams that stretched for miles, horns blaring endlessly. Rahul's back ached, his palms felt numb, and his stomach growled, but he pushed through. He learned to ignore the blistering pain in his shoulders from carrying a heavy bag all day.

By night, his body was heavy, his mind blank. But the app always pinged. Another delivery. Another call. And every time, Rahul forced himself to answer. Because this wasn't just a job anymore. This was a promise—to himself, to his family.

8

On that particular evening, as clouds gathered over the city, Rahul delivered an order near a high-rise building just as the first drops of rain began to fall. He looked up at the sky, the air cool for the first time that day, and wondered if he should head home. Then his phone buzzed.

Surge pricing: 2.5x.

Rahul hesitated, the extra pay teasing him. Finally, he straightened his back, adjusted his cap, and set off again.

The rain came down in sheets. Streets turned into rivers, and puddles splashed up to soak his legs. But the money made it worth it. Each completed order felt like a small win. He didn't mind the rain as much anymore. For the first time that day, he hummed a tune under his breath, his motorcycle cutting through the wet darkness, the headlights glinting off the slick road.

When the storm softened into a drizzle, Rahul decided to call it a day. His body screamed for rest, but his heart felt a little lighter.

His final delivery led him to a quiet lane lined with rain-soaked trees. The calm felt out of place—too still, too far removed from the chaos he had been battling all day. He handed over the food and turned his motorcycle toward home.

The streets were empty now, except for the faint buzz of streetlights and the occasional rickshaw passing by. The rain left everything shining under the yellow glow. Rahul rode slowly, his hands slacking on the handlebars.

And then he saw a figure lying by the roadside.

His grip on the brakes tightened instinctively. The motorcycle slowed, its headlight casting a pale beam on the figure.

Rahul sat frozen, the hum of the motorcycle engine vibrating under him. He took a slow, shaky breath. His eyes stayed fixed on the man, his mind racing.

9

Rahul switched off the engine, his fingers lingering on the keys. A moment passed, heavy and still. Taking a slow breath, he stepped off the motorcycle and approached the figure lying by the road.

The man was curled on his side, his face hidden by an arm. Rahul bent down, squinting in the pale light.

"Anna, are you okay?" His voice was steady, cautious.

Before he could blink, the man's hand shot up, grabbing for his neck. Rahul jerked back, stumbling a step. The man cursed under his breath, springing to his feet like a coiled spring unwinding.

Rahul barely had time to process when he heard the scuff of footsteps behind him. He spun around. A second man emerged from the shadows, gripping a metal rod that gleamed faintly under the streetlight.

The rod sliced through the air. Rahul ducked instinctively, his pulse hammering in his ears. The whoosh of metal missing his head by inches left him frozen for a heartbeat.

The first man joined in, circling to Rahul's left. The two thieves exchanged a quick glance, their movements deliberate, practiced.

Rahul clenched his fists, his body tensed. He wasn't fast enough to dodge when the second thief lunged again, the rod striking toward his ribs. He raised his delivery bag just in time, the impact reverberating through his arm.

Rahul twisted, using the bag as a shield to deflect the next swing. Without thinking, he drove his fist forward, connecting with the first thief's jaw. The man staggered back, his hands flailing to find balance.

The second man hesitated, eyes darting between Rahul and his fallen companion. Rahul seized the moment, stepping forward and landing a sharp kick to the second man's shin. A strangled yell escaped him as he crumpled, clutching his leg.

Rahul's breaths came fast and sharp, rain dripping from his cap and pooling at his feet. His muscles screamed with exhaustion, but he forced himself to stay upright.

The first man recovered quickly, rage flickering in his eyes. He charged at Rahul, shoving him hard in the chest. The world tilted as Rahul fell back onto the wet asphalt, the impact knocking the air from his lungs.

The second thief, limping slightly, scrambled toward Rahul's motorcycle. The engine roared to life as he swung a leg over the seat.

"Rey!" Rahul shouted, his voice cracking as he scrambled to his feet.

By the time Rahul pushed himself up, the motorcycle was already disappearing, its red tail light shrinking into the distance.

Rahul sprinted after it, his shoes slapping against the wet road, but the pain in his legs and the fading taillight told him it was futile. He stopped, drenched and heaving, fury bubbling to the surface.

His fists clenched. His roar echoed through the night—a cry of anger and defeat that broke the stillness of the empty street.

BEAST MODE
UNLEASHED

10

For a moment, Rahul stood there, chest heaving, rainwater dripping from his hair. The fight may have been lost, but something had shifted within him. His body trembled from exhaustion, yet anger simmered just below the surface. The image of his stolen motorcycle flashed in his mind, taunting him.

The distant sound of rain against the pavement filled the silence. Rahul staggered to a lamppost, leaning heavily against its cold metal surface. His breath came in ragged bursts, ribs aching with every sharp inhale. He reached into his pocket and pulled out his phone, the screen slick with water and grime. His thumb hovered over the contacts, hesitating.

The street was empty, shadows deepening with the relentless drizzle. Helplessness gnawed at him. He clenched his jaw and scrolled down, landing on Sanjay's name.

The phone rang, cutting through the night's quiet. Each ring stretched longer than the last, until Sanjay's voice finally crackled through. "Hello? Rahul, what's up?"

"Sanjay..." Rahul's voice cracked. He swallowed hard, forcing the words out. "Phase 4, Road No. 3. Come quick."

Sanjay's tone shifted instantly. "What happened? Are you okay?"

"Just come," Rahul snapped, his frustration spilling over before the line disconnected.

Back at home, Sanjay shoved on his jacket and kick-started his father's old scooter. The engine sputtered to life as he muttered, "Rahul, what kind of mess have you gotten yourself into this time?"

11

As Sanjay reached the road Rahul had described, his headlights cut through the misty drizzle, illuminating a lone figure under the flickering streetlights. Rahul's shoulders were hunched, fists clenched so tightly his knuckles turned white. Rain streamed from his soaked clothes, his steps sluggish yet purposeful, like a man weighed down by fury and exhaustion.

"Rahul!" Sanjay called out, his voice sharp with concern. He stopped the scooter abruptly, nearly skidding on the slick road before jumping off. "What the hell happened? You look like you just went twelve rounds with a street gang."

Rahul exhaled sharply, his breath unsteady. His jaw worked as if forcing the words out. "I—I stopped to help someone. Thought he was hurt. He wasn't."

Sanjay's brow furrowed. "What?"

Rahul's voice came faster, each word laced with frustration. "It was a setup. He grabbed me. Then another guy came from behind. They hit me, stole my motorcycle, and disappeared into the night."

Sanjay's face darkened, his fingers twitching at his sides. "You mean to tell me—" his voice rose, "—that you just got mugged? And we're standing here like idiots instead of chasing them?!"

Rahul thrust a shaking hand toward a shadowy street. "That way."

Sanjay didn't hesitate. "Get on." He gripped the scooter's handlebars like a man about to charge into battle.

Rahul swung onto the back without another word. Sanjay stomped on the kick-start. The scooter coughed. Spluttered. Died.

Silence hung between them. Rahul closed his eyes briefly. Sanjay gritted his teeth. He kicked again. Nothing. Again. Still nothing.

"Unbelievable," Sanjay muttered, shaking his head. "Come on, you stubborn pile of junk!"

He tilted the scooter sharply to one side, earning an incredulous look from Rahul. "What are you doing?"

"Fuel shift trick," Sanjay replied, his voice thick with mock wisdom. "This old girl needs a little encouragement."

Rahul exhaled through his nose, visibly restraining himself. "Encouragement?"

Sanjay straightened up and kicked again, harder this time. The scooter wheezed like an asthmatic cat.

Rahul swiped a hand over his face. "Move." He got off, nudged Sanjay aside, and slammed the kick-start twice. The engine roared to life like it had been waiting for him all along.

Sanjay wasted no time hopping on. "Yeah, okay, okay." He clamped onto Rahul's shoulders as the scooter lurched forward.

The road ahead stretched like a black void, streetlights glinting off the slick pavement. Rahul's grip tightened around the handlebars, his knuckles pale in the dim glow. His anger burned low and deep, smoldering beneath his skin.

"They're gone, man," Sanjay muttered over his shoulder. "Unless they stopped somewhere for a tea break, we're not catching them."

Rahul's jaw set. The scooter hummed beneath them, the cold air biting at their wet skin. "We'll see about that," he murmured, pushing the throttle harder.

12

The scooter hummed along the empty street, the rain now a gentle mist clinging to their jackets. Sanjay sighed, breaking the silence. "Look, bro. It's late. You're hurt. And honestly, I don't think they're waiting around for us to catch up."

Rahul didn't respond, his knuckles whitening as he gripped the handlebars tighter. His mind replayed the events of the night—the fight, the thieves, the sharp sting of fists slamming into his ribs, the moment his motorcycle disappeared into the rain-soaked darkness.

Sanjay shifted slightly, his tone softening. "I get it. It's your motorcycle. I'd be losing my mind too. But you can't do anything tonight. Let's head back, file a police report tomorrow. We'll figure this out, okay?"

Rahul slowed the scooter to a stop. The drizzle picked up again, tiny drops sliding down his head. He stared down the road, unwilling to turn back, his heart heavy with frustration. His eyes scanned the shadows one last time, hoping for something.

But finally, he let out a long breath. "Fine," he muttered, his voice barely audible.

Without another word, he turned the scooter around. The ride home was silent, the hum of the engine the only sound between them. Sanjay sat quietly, giving Rahul space to process.

13

The next morning, the air was crisp, carrying a faint chill that Rahul barely noticed as he and Sanjay stepped into the police station. The moment they entered, a wave of noise hit him like a wall. Complainants argued in hushed yet urgent voices, officers moved briskly between desks, and the sharp clatter of files being shuffled punctuated the chaos. The smell of stale coffee and old paper hung in the air, mixing with the occasional waft of sweat.

Rahul's fingers brushed nervously against his jeans, his palms already damp. He had never been inside a police station before, and the sheer intensity of the place made his stomach churn. He had imagined this moment in his head—walking in, explaining what happened, demanding action—but now, standing amidst the controlled chaos, he felt small.

Sanjay, however, seemed unfazed. He walked with an easy confidence, his voice cutting through the din.

"Excuse me, sir! We want to file a complaint," he called to an officer who was halfway out the door.

The officer barely slowed, pointing toward a desk without looking back. "Go over there," he muttered, vanishing into the crowd.

Rahul followed Sanjay's lead, weaving through the room's chaotic energy to the indicated desk. A middle-aged inspector sat there, his nameplate reading **Inspector Ramana**. His sleeves were rolled up, revealing tanned forearms, and he was deep in conversation with another man, his hands moving animatedly as he spoke.

Sanjay cleared his throat loudly. "Sir, we need to file a complaint."

Ramana's gaze flicked upward, sharp and dismissive. He exhaled through his nose, then pointed to a nearby bench. "Sit there. I'll call you in five minutes." His voice was clipped, his focus already shifting back to his discussion.

Rahul sank onto the bench, his shoulders stiff, his hands clasped tightly together. His mind replayed the events of the previous night—the fight, the thieves, the helplessness that lingered like a shadow. His stomach knotted as he imagined his father's reaction when he found out about the stolen motorcycle. He hadn't told his family yet. He didn't have the heart to.

Beside him, Sanjay leaned back, his foot tapping lightly against the floor, his gaze sweeping the room like they had all the time in the world.

"Dude, the inspector's calling us," Sanjay whispered, nudging Rahul back into the present.

Rahul's pulse quickened as he stood, his footsteps feeling heavy as they approached the desk. Inspector Ramana gestured for them to sit, pulling a fresh sheet of paper from a stack and readying his pen.

"Tell me what happened," Ramana said, his voice businesslike.

Rahul took a deep breath, steadying himself. "I lost my motorcycle, sir. Last night around 2 A.M., two thieves attacked me and stole it."

Ramana's pen paused briefly before his sharp gaze fixed on Rahul. "Why were you out at that time?"

Rahul's throat felt dry, but he kept his voice even. "I do food delivery," he replied, sensing Sanjay shift beside him. He kept his focus on Ramana, refusing to glance away.

"Why at night?" Ramana pressed.

"There's a surge in pay at night," Rahul explained, the words feeling rehearsed. "In the morning, I go to college."

Ramana clicked his tongue, shaking his head slightly. "Why don't you focus on your studies and get a better job? These delivery jobs are not good for your future."

Rahul's hands tightened in his lap. He had heard this before—from professors, neighbors, even some relatives. They said it like he had a choice, like his life wasn't dictated by necessity.

"Sir, I need the money," he said, his voice firm but polite. "My dad met with an accident recently, and I'm doing this temporarily to support my family."

Ramana exhaled, rubbing his temple for a moment. When he looked back at Rahul, his expression had softened—just slightly. He nodded once and began filling out the FIR, the pen scratching steadily across the page.

"Fine. Give me the details."

Rahul recounted the events of the night in detail, his voice steady even as his chest tightened with frustration. Ramana occasionally glanced up to clarify, his sharp eyes missing nothing.

Finally, the inspector handed Rahul a slip of paper. "We'll inform you when we find your motorcycle," he said, leaning back in his chair.

Rahul hesitated, his words catching in his throat. "Sir, is there any chance I could get it back in a day or two? I really need that motorcycle. I haven't even told my family about this yet."

Ramana studied Rahul for a long moment, his expression unreadable. "I understand your situation, but these things take time. Send me a photo of the motorcycle. Do you have one?"

Rahul nodded quickly, pulling out his phone. His fingers trembled slightly as he unlocked it, scrolling to find a picture. He handed it to Ramana, who entered his number into it.

"Send the details to this number," the inspector said, returning the phone. "We'll do our best."

"Thank you, inspector," Rahul said, sincerity thick in his voice as he rose to his feet. Sanjay followed, offering Ramana a quick nod before they left.

As they stepped outside, Rahul inhaled deeply, the cold air filling his lungs. He wanted to believe Ramana's words, but doubt lingered.

14

Outside, the morning sun shone brightly, but its warmth did little to lift the weight pressing on Rahul's shoulders. He took a deep breath, the crisp air biting against his skin. As they walked away from the police station, the image of his dad sitting silently in the hospital bed replayed in his mind. The guilt of failing him only added to the knot in his chest.

Sanjay walked beside him, hands in his pockets, his usual carefree demeanor slightly subdued. "Look, man, the cops will do their thing, but we both know how slow these things go."

Rahul exhaled sharply. "I can't afford to wait. I need that motorcycle. Without it, I can't work, and without work..." He trailed off, the weight of reality pressing down on him.

Sanjay gave him a measured look before nodding. "Alright!"

Rahul ran a hand through his hair, thinking. "The place where it happened. Maybe someone saw something—security cameras, street vendors, night guards. There has to be something."

The two changed direction, heading toward the dimly lit alley where Rahul had been ambushed. The streets were alive with the sounds of morning—vendors calling out their wares, cyclists weaving through the light traffic, the occasional honk of an impatient driver. But beneath the normalcy, Rahul felt the hum of his own desperation.

15

Under the dim, flickering light of a wood factory tucked away on the outskirts of the city, Vijay and Ravi worked in tense silence, loading motorcycles into an old, dented van. The air smelled of sawdust and oil, a lingering mix that clung to their clothes.

Ravi adjusted his gloves, his brow furrowed. "Last night was different," he muttered under his breath.

Vijay didn't look up, tightening the straps around one of the motorcycles. "Yeah, but we got the motorcycle. That's what matters."

"That kid," Ravi growled, fists tightening. "The delivery guy. He fought back." His jaw clenched as he turned suddenly, slamming his fist against the van. The dull thud echoed through the warehouse. "No one fights back."

From the other side of the warehouse, Ramesh, a wiry man with a cocky smirk, overheard the conversation. Unable to resist, he swaggered closer. "If I'd been there," he boasted, rolling his shoulders, "that kid wouldn't have gotten away. I'd have put him down."

For a moment, Ravi just stared, breathing hard. Then, in a flash, he grabbed Ramesh by the neck and shoved him against the wall. "You think you're better than me, huh?" His voice was a low growl. "Let's see you handle someone fighting back next time."

Ramesh flinched, his confidence crumbling as he struggled against Ravi's grip. "Alright, alright! Let me go!"

"Enough." Vijay's sharp voice cut through the tension. He stepped between them, yanking Ravi back with a firm grip. "We don't have time for this." His eyes darted between the two men, hard and unyielding. "Get back to work. We've got a shipment to move, and we can't afford slip-ups."

The warehouse fell silent, save for the faint hum of distant machinery.

Vijay's voice dropped, his words edged with warning. "Listen up. Keep your heads down and stay out of trouble for the next few days. Karan says the heat's on, and we can't risk anything going sideways before the deal. No mistakes. No delays. No excuses."

Ramesh muttered something under his breath but didn't argue. Ravi exhaled sharply, stepping away, but his fists remained clenched.

16

The hardware shop was cramped and dimly lit, the air thick with the scent of machine oil and rust. Tools and spare parts cluttered the shelves, casting long, jagged shadows across the cracked floor. Sunny stepped inside, his sharp gaze sweeping over the place before settling on the gray-haired shopkeeper hunched behind the counter.

The shopkeeper barely glanced up, his frame stiffening at the sight of a stranger. Sunny moved closer, flipping open his ID with a practiced ease.

"Inspector Sunny," he said. "I need last night's CCTV footage. There was an incident reported here."

The shopkeeper squinted at the ID, his fingers tapping idly on the counter. "No uniform, no police jeep," he muttered. "Anyone can print an ID these days."

Sunny smirked, tilting his head slightly. His hand slipped into his jacket, the air between them tightening like a drawn wire. A sleek black pistol appeared in his grip, held steady but not quite threatening—just a silent, undeniable fact.

"How about this for proof?" His voice was dangerously calm.

The shopkeeper stiffened, his throat bobbing in a nervous swallow. "Alright, alright! No need for all that, officer. Can't be too careful these days, you know?"

Sunny tucked the pistol back into his jacket, his smirk barely fading. "Good. Now, show me the footage."

With a muttered curse, the shopkeeper shuffled towards the back room, leading Sunny to a rickety desk with an old computer humming softly. The screen flickered, sluggish as it woke. The shopkeeper typed quickly, bringing up the footage.

"Funny thing," he murmured as he worked. "Two boys came by an hour ago, asking for the same thing. Looked shady, so I sent them off."

Sunny's brow lifted slightly. "Shady how?"

The shopkeeper shrugged. "Didn't stick around long enough to find out. But they were persistent. Seemed like they really needed it."

Sunny filed the information away as the shopkeeper stepped aside, gesturing to the screen. "There you go."

Without a word, Sunny pulled out a pen drive and plugged it in. His movements were precise, unhurried. As the files copied over, he leaned against the desk, his gaze locked on the monitor.

"Delete today's footage," he said, almost casually. "Can't have anyone knowing I was here. Undercover work, you understand."

The shopkeeper hesitated for a beat before nodding, his fingers moving over the keyboard. A few clicks later, the day's recordings were gone.

Sunny straightened, giving the man a firm pat on the shoulder. "Good man. If you ever need anything, drop by the station. Even if I'm not there, someone will help you."

The shopkeeper exhaled shakily, nodding as Sunny pocketed the pen drive and strode out. The faint clink of his boots faded into the street, leaving behind only the quiet hum of the computer and the shopkeeper's slow, steadying breaths.

17

Sunny strolled into Sanjay's place like he owned it, a duffel bag slung over his shoulder and that signature smirk firmly in place. Rahul glanced up from his seat while Sanjay merely raised an eyebrow. Sunny began unloading his props onto the table: an assortment of bizarre gadgets, fake IDs, and a highly questionable mustache. Rahul drummed his fingers impatiently, still fuming over the morning's failure.

The shopkeeper's glare replayed in his mind, cold and unwavering. "I don't know anything. No cameras here. Leave." The door slam had echoed in his ears as they walked away, empty-handed.

"We need help," Sanjay had muttered then. A moment later, his face lit up. "I know a guy."

And now, that "guy" was here, twirling a fake badge between his fingers like this was some crime drama. "Alright, boys," Sunny declared, flashing a cocky grin. "Let's catch these thieves."

Sanjay plugged a pen drive into his laptop, and the room fell silent as the footage started rolling. Sunny leaned in over his shoulder, scanning the timestamps with a practiced eye. Rahul sat beside them, his focus locked onto the screen.

"Pause here," Sunny instructed, his voice sharp. The screen froze, displaying two shadowy figures speeding off on Rahul's stolen motorcycle.

"They're heading down this road," Sunny said, tapping a spot on the map on his phone. "And... here. It ends."

The footage cut off just as the thieves veered into a narrow alleyway.

Rahul's frustration boiled over. "Uncle, what now? That was our only lead!"

Sunny leaned back, smirking. "You can call me bro, kid. Sounds cooler."

Rahul slammed his fist on the table, causing both of them to jump. "The footage ends here, and we've got nothing!" He pointed at the map on Sunny's phone. "This area—we need footage from here. It's our only shot!"

Sanjay frowned, rubbing his chin. "That's a residential zone. No CCTVs. I've tried."

Rahul slumped back, hands covering his face. "This was it. We almost had them."

Sunny sighed, stretching his arms lazily behind his head. "Relax, kid. There's always another way. Sometimes, you just have to—" He mimed pulling a trigger. "Persuade people."

"Nothing illegal." Sunny's grin didn't fade. "Just a little creative interrogation."

A sharp knock on the door cut through the tension.

Sanjay exchanged a look with Rahul. "Who could that be?"

"Think it's the thieves?"

"No. Worse."

Sunny stood, motioning for them to stay put. He opened the door to find a stern-faced police officer standing beside the shopkeeper from earlier.

"That's him!" the shopkeeper burst out, jabbing a finger at Sunny. "He's the one, officer!"

Sunny raised an eyebrow, unfazed. "The one what?"

The officer gave him a once-over. "We got a complaint. Impersonating a police officer, threatening a shopkeeper—"

Rahul and Sanjay exchanged wide-eyed glances.

Sunny let out a low chuckle, hands raised in mock surrender. "Let's not jump to conclusions, Officer."

The shopkeeper wasn't having it. "He pointed a gun at me! Made me delete footage!"

Rahul's heart pounded as the officer stepped inside, handcuffs dangling from his belt. Sunny, still infuriatingly calm, leaned against the doorframe.

"Gentlemen," he said smoothly, flashing that ever-present grin, "I think there's been a tiny misunderstanding."

18

In the police station, phones rang, officers moved swiftly, and the air carried a mix of urgency and indifference. Sunny, Sanjay, and Rahul sat on a bench across from Inspector Ramana's desk. The inspector looked up from a file, his brow furrowed as he fixed his gaze on Sunny.

"You're a grown man," Ramana said, his tone firm but not unkind. "Why are you encouraging these kids to run around like this?"

Sunny opened his mouth to respond, but Ramana raised a hand to stop him.

"I don't want to hear it. And you two"—he turned to Rahul and Sanjay—"stay out of it. This is a police matter. You'll only get yourselves into trouble."

Rahul lowered his gaze, but Sanjay stood abruptly. "Yes, sir."

Ramana gestured toward a man sitting quietly on a bench nearby. He had a lean frame, unshaven stubble, and a worn expression.

"See him?" the inspector asked. "That's Arjun. He lost his motorcycle just like you did a week ago. There are others too. We're working on these cases, so don't worry—we'll do our best."

Rahul glanced at Ramana, then at the man. As Ramana's words settled, he stood and walked toward Arjun, determination setting in with each step.

"Hi, I'm Rahul," he said, extending a hand.

The man looked up, startled at first, then shook Rahul's hand.

"Arjun," he replied, his voice tired.

"I heard you lost your motorcycle," Rahul said. "Do you think you could show me the spot?"

Arjun frowned, his eyes narrowing slightly. "Why?"

"We're trying to track down the same gang," Rahul said simply. "They took my motorcycle last night."

Arjun hesitated, then leaned in closer to Rahul, his voice barely above a whisper. "I've been looking into it myself. I think I've found a suspicious place."

19

The small chai shop buzzed with the usual evening chatter. Steam curled from cups lined along the counter, mingling with the aroma of freshly fried pakoras. Rahul, Arjun, and Sanjay sat at a cramped table, their chai cooling as the conversation turned serious.

"I was riding home late after work," Arjun began, his voice steady but laced with frustration. "I saw someone lying on the road. When I went to check on him, he suddenly grabbed my neck. Another guy came from behind. They beat me up and stole my motorcycle."

Rahul sat up, his brows knitting together. "The same thing happened to me last night. Exactly the same."

Sanjay, lounging back, took a sip of chai and shrugged. "Why worry? The police will find it soon. Besides, you still have another ride." He gestured toward a battered scooter parked outside.

Arjun's expression darkened. His fingers tightened around the chai glass. "That motorcycle belonged to my dad. It's all I have left of him. He served in the military."

Rahul's gaze dropped. Guilt settled over him. His voice softened. "Damn, man. I'm sorry. We didn't know."

Sanjay straightened, suddenly more serious. "Yeah, bro. We had no idea."

Arjun shook his head. "It's fine."

Sanjay leaned forward and pulled out his phone. "Check this out. We got some CCTV footage."

Arjun took the phone, his jaw clenching as he watched the grainy video. "Damn. That's them."

Rahul leaned in. "Where exactly did they take your motorcycle? If we get more footage, we might be able to track them."

Arjun hesitated before answering. "I did some digging. Found out about a mechanic shop—more like a front for stolen motorcycles."

Sanjay raised an eyebrow. "You sure?"

Arjun nodded. "I got some help from guys who run with local gangs."

Rahul cut in before Sanjay could respond. "Doesn't matter. Where's the place?"

Arjun tapped his fingers on the table. "I went there once. They warned me to stay away. Said if I showed up again, they'd make sure I regretted it."

Rahul exchanged a look with Sanjay and then he pushed his chair back and stood. "Let's go."

He glanced at Sanjay. "Pay for the chai."

Sanjay held up his hands. "I'm broke."

Rahul frowned. "You had money this morning. I gave you some."

Sanjay smirked and reached into his bag, pulling out a small black object. "I paid Sunny, but he didn't have change, so I took this."

Rahul stared. "A prop gun? What the hell are we supposed to do with this?".

Then Sanjay walked up to the chaiwala. "Forgot my wallet. I'll pay you in the evening."

The shopkeeper grabbed his shirt, eyes narrowing. "No credit. Pay now."

With an easy grin, Sanjay raised the prop gun, waving it lazily. The shopkeeper's grip loosened, his face turning pale.

"I swear, I'll pay you later," Sanjay said smoothly.

The shopkeeper hesitated before stepping back. "Okay, anna. No problem."

Sanjay nodded and turned to the others. "Let's go."

"What the hell are you doing, man?" Rahul asked, his voice low but sharp. He stood beside Sanjay, his expression tense.

Rahul sighed and gave the shopkeeper an apologetic glance as they stepped outside.

20

The sun hung high, casting sharp shadows as Rahul, Arjun, and Sanjay stood across the street from the mechanic shop. The metallic clang of tools and the faint hum of passing vehicles filled the air. Sanjay shifted uneasily, glancing at the few people loitering in the area.

"Are you sure, man?" he muttered to Rahul, his voice barely above a whisper. "This area looks... you know, not good."

Rahul's gaze didn't waver from the shop. His jaw tightened as he adjusted his grip on the phone in his pocket. "You stay outside. If anything goes wrong, call the cops."

Sanjay hesitated, his eyes darting between Rahul and the shop. "Just don't do anything stupid, okay?"

Rahul nodded curtly and crossed the road with Arjun. The shop's corrugated iron walls were streaked with grime, and the air smelled of grease and burnt oil. Rahul's pulse quickened, his instincts screaming danger.

Inside, a group of men sat on mismatched chairs, their voices cutting off mid-sentence as Rahul and Arjun entered. One of the men, Swamy, stood up slowly, his eyes narrowing as recognition flickered.

"You came back?" Swamy's voice was low, a threat simmering beneath it. His steps were deliberate as he approached.

Rahul's muscles tensed. He clenched his fists, his heartbeat hammering in his ears. Beside him, Arjun shifted uneasily, his hesitation palpable. But Rahul didn't falter.

Swamy reached for Rahul's collar. Time seemed to slow. Rahul's fist moved first, connecting with Swamy's ribs. The sickening thud echoed in the room, and Swamy crumpled into a chair, groaning as he clutched his side.

The room froze. All eyes locked on Rahul.

Arjun edged back, his shoulders hunching. Another man, tall and broad-shouldered, stepped forward, fury etched across his face. "How dare you hit our man?"

The man swung at Rahul. For a heartbeat, everything slowed again. Rahul ducked instinctively, his movements sharp and fluid. He caught the man's arm mid-swing and shoved him hard into a stack of tires. The tires toppled, the clatter breaking the fragile silence.

The room erupted. Men surged forward, their movements chaotic. Rahul braced himself, adrenaline flooding his veins. Each strike he landed felt instinctive yet deliberate—an elbow to the ribs, a fist to the jaw, a kick to the stomach. The sharp crack of fists meeting flesh reverberated through the grimy walls.

Swamy, still wheezing, fumbled in his pocket and pulled out a knife. Rahul caught the glint of the blade in the dim light. His heart lurched, but he held his ground, his fists ready.

"Stop!"

The shout came from the doorway. Sanjay stood there, the prop gun gripped tightly in both hands, its barrel trembling but aimed at Swamy. Sanjay's knuckles were white, his chest heaving. His voice broke the chaos. "Look, I've got a terrible aim. Wanna try?"

Swamy froze. His eyes darted between the knife and the gun, calculating. Slowly, the blade slipped from his fingers, clattering to the floor.

"The motorcycles are in the backyard," Swamy grunted, raising his hands in surrender.

Rahul exhaled sharply, the tension in his shoulders easing just enough to let him move. He gestured to Arjun, who stumbled forward, his movements stiff and uncertain. Together, they stepped into the yard.

21

Outside, the yard stretched before them, a graveyard of stripped motorcycles and dusty frames. The air was heavy with the smell of rust and oil, and the faint buzz of a distant generator hummed through the silence.

Rahul scanned the rows, his chest tightening with every step. His gaze darted from one broken frame to the next, each empty shell hammering home a bitter truth: their motorcycles weren't there.

Behind him, Sanjay still stood by the doorway, the prop gun dangling loosely in his grip. "Well," he muttered, his voice heavy with sarcasm, "at least we found enough scrap metal to start a recycling business."

Rahul's jaw tightened as disappointment coursed through him. His fists clenched at his sides, the frustration threatening to boil over. Without a word, he turned and marched back into the shop.

He pulled out his phone, holding the CCTV footage in front of Swamy. "Where is this motorcycle?" Rahul demanded, his voice low and firm.

Swamy leaned back, his expression unreadable. "We don't attack people and steal, man," he said, his tone calm but pointed. "We just take parked ones—places where there's no CCTV."

Rahul's fists tightened, the chaos and effort feeling like a cruel joke. "I'm sorry," he muttered, his voice tight.

As they turned to leave, Swamy clapped once, the sound sharp and deliberate. Rahul paused, his head turning slightly.

Swamy rubbed his ribs, a strange glint in his eye. "That guy in the footage, I've seen him near Ranga's wine shop once. Familiar face, but I can't say for sure."

Arjun nodded stiffly. "Thanks."

Swamy's voice followed them out, dripping with menace. "If I ever see you in this area again, I won't let you go."

They left quickly, their steps heavy with frustration. Sanjay fell into step beside them, twirling the prop gun idly.

Inside the shop, one of Swamy's men frowned. "Anna, why'd you let them go?"

Swamy chuckled darkly, wincing as he straightened in his chair. A malicious grin spread across his face.

"That guy in the picture…" he said slowly, "he's with Deva's gang." His laughter grew louder, bouncing off the walls.

22

In Sanjay's cluttered room, Arjun sat on a rickety chair, arms folded, while Rahul and Sanjay perched on the bed. Rahul's gaze was fixed on the laptop screen, scanning through the CCTV footage again and flipping between map tabs, zooming in on Ranga's wine shop.

Sanjay broke the silence, trying to sound casual, but unease crept into his tone. "C'mon, man. Why don't we just leave this to the police? This is getting way more dangerous than we thought. What if those guys figured out it was a prop gun? They could've stabbed you, Rahul!"

Rahul barely glanced up, his fingers tightening around the laptop. "We're so close," he said firmly. "We almost got them."

Sanjay threw up his hands. "Almost got killed, you mean!"

The words cut through the room. Rahul snapped the laptop shut with a sharp click and turned to Sanjay, his jaw set. "Nothing happened, man. Why are you so scared?"

Sanjay leaned forward, his voice rising. "I saved you from being stabbed! If I hadn't stepped in, who knows what would've happened?"

He pointed toward Arjun, who had been quietly observing the exchange, his arms still folded. "Ask him! He was there too."

Arjun hesitated, his gaze dropping to the floor. "Rahul, maybe Sanjay's right."

Rahul stood abruptly, making the bed creak under the sudden movement. His frustration spilled over. "We'll try one last time. If this doesn't work—"

Sanjay scoffed, shaking his head. "Yeah, right."

Rahul's eyes flashed with irritation. "Fine! This time, I'll go alone."

Without another word, he strode out of the room, the door slamming shut behind him. The sound echoed through the small apartment, leaving a heavy silence in its wake.

Arjun turned to Sanjay, concern etched on his face. "It's not a good idea letting him go alone."

Sanjay flopped onto the bed and stared at the ceiling. "He's stubborn. You've seen it. Once he decides something, there's no stopping him."

Rahul's footsteps faded down the hallway as he left the building. Sanjay sat up, rubbing his temples. He groaned dramatically before shouting after him, his voice dripping with sarcasm, "Hey, hero! Don't forget to save the day!"

23

The open area behind the wine shop buzzed with noise—clinking bottles, raucous laughter, and the occasional curse drifting through the smoky air. Rahul and Arjun wove through the clusters of people, ignoring the wary stares and hushed whispers. Arjun held up his phone, showing a grainy CCTV image to anyone willing to look.

"Seen this guy?" he asked a man nursing a glass of whiskey at a makeshift table.

The man glanced at the photo and grunted. "No idea." He turned back to his drink, dismissing them.

Rahul tried another. "Do you know this guy?"

A man smirked. "You the police?"

"No, but—"

Before Rahul could finish, the wine shop's owner stormed out, his face flushed with irritation. "What the hell is going on here?" he bellowed, silencing the chatter. His sharp gaze flickered between Rahul and Arjun. "You're disturbing my customers. Take your nonsense somewhere else!"

"We're just.." Arjun said, his voice steady.

The owner stepped closer, his tone turning sharper, more dangerous. "Don't test my patience. Leave. Now."

Rahul's fists clenched, his knuckles whitening. Just as the tension thickened, an older man from the crowd intervened. He placed a firm hand on the owner's shoulder. "C'mon man, They're just kids."

The owner clicked his tongue and spat near a trash fire flickering close to the wall. "Don't show your faces here again." With one last glare, he spun on his heel and stomped back inside, muttering curses under his breath.

As the crowd dispersed, Rahul and Arjun turned to leave. That's when Arjun noticed a man seated in the corner, a glass of whiskey in hand. He wasn't focused on his drink—his sharp eyes followed their every move.

"Rahul," Arjun murmured, slowing his pace. "That guy's watching us."

"What guy?" Rahul asked, scanning the area.

The man had just averted his gaze, his movements deliberate, as he set his glass down and stood up.

"He's leaving," Arjun muttered. Without waiting, he quickened his pace, shadowing the man as he slipped out of the noisy crowd into a side alley.

The narrow lane reeked of damp cement and burnt trash. Smoke curled from a nearby fire, creating a hazy curtain that blurred the path ahead. The man—Ramesh—walked briskly, his head slightly tilted, as if listening for footsteps behind him.

Arjun's heart pounded. He kept his steps light, careful not to be noticed. But as they neared a bend where the smoke thickened, the man disappeared.

"Where did he go?" Rahul asked, catching up, his voice tight with frustration.

"He was right here," Arjun muttered, scanning the alley, his eyes narrowing at the flickering shadows shifting in the haze.

24

The dimly lit wooden factory buzzed with tension as Ramesh approached a group of men gathered near a workbench. Among them were Vijay and Ravi. Ramesh, catching his breath, gestured frantically toward the door.

"Those boys are asking around the area. I barely got away, and I told Karan" he said, his voice low and urgent.

"You called Karan?" Ravi snapped, his expression turning dark.

"Yes. I thought—"

"You thought wrong!" Ravi barked, cutting him off. "We can handle this. Why bring Karan into it? And why are you drinking in the afternoon?"

Before Ramesh could defend himself, the sound of footsteps echoed through the factory. Everyone turned as Rahul, Arjun, and Sanjay stepped in through the main door. Without a word, Rahul grabbed the handle and turned the lock with a decisive click.

Earlier that day, As Sanjay had stubbornly refused to join Rahul and Arjun, dismissing their plan as reckless. But curiosity gnawed at him. When they headed to the wine shop, he trailed them at a distance, watching as Rahul confronted Ramesh. The heated argument spilled into the alley, ending with Ramesh bolting in a panic.

Sanjay didn't stop to think. Staying in the shadows, he followed Ramesh through winding streets and dark corners. His pulse quickened when the man slipped into a wooden factory. Sanjay crouched low, edging closer until he found a hiding spot behind a stack of crates. From there, he waited, listening as muffled voices filled the space. His fingers flew over his phone, sending Rahul a quick message: "I'm following the whisky unfinished guy."

Moments later, Rahul and Arjun arrived outside the factory. Sanjay stepped out of his hiding place and joined them, the three exchanging a nod before entering together.

The room fell silent as the three boys entered. Rahul turned back to the group, a sly smile spreading across his face.

"You remember me, guys?" Rahul asked, his voice calm but laced with mockery. "We met yesterday."

He turned his gaze to Vijay, who stiffened under the scrutiny.

"You," Rahul said, pointing a finger at him, "you're wasting your talent. That performance last night? Great acting. Really had me fooled."

Vijay clenched his fists but stayed silent as Ravi and the others exchanged uneasy glances. Six more men, all part of the gang, emerged from different corners of the factory, standing in a loose circle around the three intruders. The air thickened with tension as the gang prepared for what might come next.

Meanwhile, at the police station, Inspector Ramana leaned back in his chair, staring at his phone. Rahul's shared location marked the wooden factory. Ramana's expression darkened as he pieced the situation together.

"These kids are running straight into trouble," he muttered, already reaching for his radio. "Get the backup team ready," he ordered his officers. "We're heading out now. Start the vehicle."

The officers sprang into action, their urgency palpable as the inspector grabbed his hat and strode out of the station.

25

Back at the factory, Rahul's fists clenched as he faced the gang members encircling them. Sanjay stood slightly behind him, his usual smirk absent, replaced by a look of cautious resolve, while Arjun's nervous glances darted between the men and the locked door.

Vijay stepped forward, his sneer cutting through the tense air.

"So, you think you can just walk in here and—"

"I didn't come here to argue," Rahul cut in, his tone even but ice-cold. "Where's my motorcycle?"

The tension snapped. One of the gang members lunged at Rahul. He sidestepped, caught the man's wrist in a tight grip, and drove a fist into his ribs. The man crumpled with a pained grunt.

"Rahul, behind you!" Sanjay's warning came just in time.

A metal pipe whistled past Rahul's head as he ducked. His pulse spiked, but his instincts took over. He countered with a swift kick to the man's knee, sending him sprawling.

Nearby, Arjun grappled with a wiry attacker throwing wild punches. He barely managed to block, stumbling backward, his breath coming in short, panicked gasps. With a desperate shove, he created a sliver of distance.

Sanjay's eyes scanned the factory. Weapons. I need something. He darted toward a stack of crates near the parked vans, crouching low. A shadow loomed over him—no time to think. He grabbed a loose wooden plank and swung blindly. The crack of wood hitting flesh made him wince, but the gang member staggered back.

"Not bad," he muttered, scrambling to his feet.

The room erupted into chaos. Heavy fists. Clanging metal. Ragged breathing.

Ravi stepped in, his punches landing with brutal precision. Rahul blocked two, gritted his teeth as a third slammed into his shoulder. Pain flared, but he ignored it, ducked under Ravi's next swing, and delivered a sharp uppercut. Ravi reeled back, shaking his head.

Two gang members armed themselves with iron rods, their eyes locked onto Rahul. Their movements were different—disciplined, precise. Not street brawlers. Fighters.

One of them swung. Rahul caught the rod mid-motion, twisting it free in a fluid motion. The second gang member lunged, but Rahul deflected the strike, then brought the rod down hard. The sharp thud of impact sent the attacker crumpling.

Arjun, still shaky, managed to land a punch—but his victory was short-lived. A boot slammed into his ribs, knocking him to the ground. Pain exploded in his side. He gasped, trying to get up, but his attacker loomed over him.

Before the gang member could land another blow, Rahul grabbed him by the collar and hurled him into a stack of crates. The wood splintered on impact, the crash echoing through the factory.

Sanjay's voice cut through the commotion.

"Guys, a little help here!"

He dodged a flying wrench, barely missing his head. Another gang member closed in fast. "Seriously!"

Then—the distant wail of sirens.

Sanjay's eyes lit up with relief. "Hear that? haha.."

The gang froze. Their confidence cracked, fear creeping in. Some bolted for the back exit, but Rahul wasn't letting Ravi go. He drove him to the ground, pinning him.

The factory doors burst open.

"Secure the perimeter!" Inspector Ramana's voice rang out. His officers spread out, moving in.

Ramana's gaze locked onto Rahul, then shifted to the parked vans. "Check them."

Rahul and Arjun rushed to the van. Their breath was heavy. Their hands shook with anticipation. They flung open the doors.

Rows of stolen motorcycles.

But not theirs.

A heavy silence settled between them.

"Where is it?" Arjun muttered, frustration thick in his voice.

Then—an engine roared outside.

A sleek black SUV screeched to a halt.

A tall man stepped out. Karan.

Everything about him demanded attention. The way he moved—deliberate, controlled, dangerous. He was already in motion before the officers could react.

Two cops moved in. Too slow.

Karan dropped the first with a swift strike to the throat, barely breaking stride. The second reached for his gun—Karan disarmed him in one fluid motion, sending him crumpling with a sharp blow to the ribs.

Ravi broke free—Rahul felt him slip from his grasp.

Karan's eyes met Rahul's for a split second. Something unreadable in that gaze. A warning? A challenge?

Then, without a word, Karan turned, sliding into the SUV with Ravi.

The vehicle roared away, tires kicking up dust as it disappeared.

Rahul stood frozen. His fists clenched tight.

"Who was that?" His voice was steady. Too steady.

Ramana's expression was grim.

"Karan. He's leading Deva's gang now."

The dust settled.

Rahul's jaw tightened. His pulse was still pounding, but now, it wasn't from the fight. It was from something else. A new resolve.

This wasn't over.

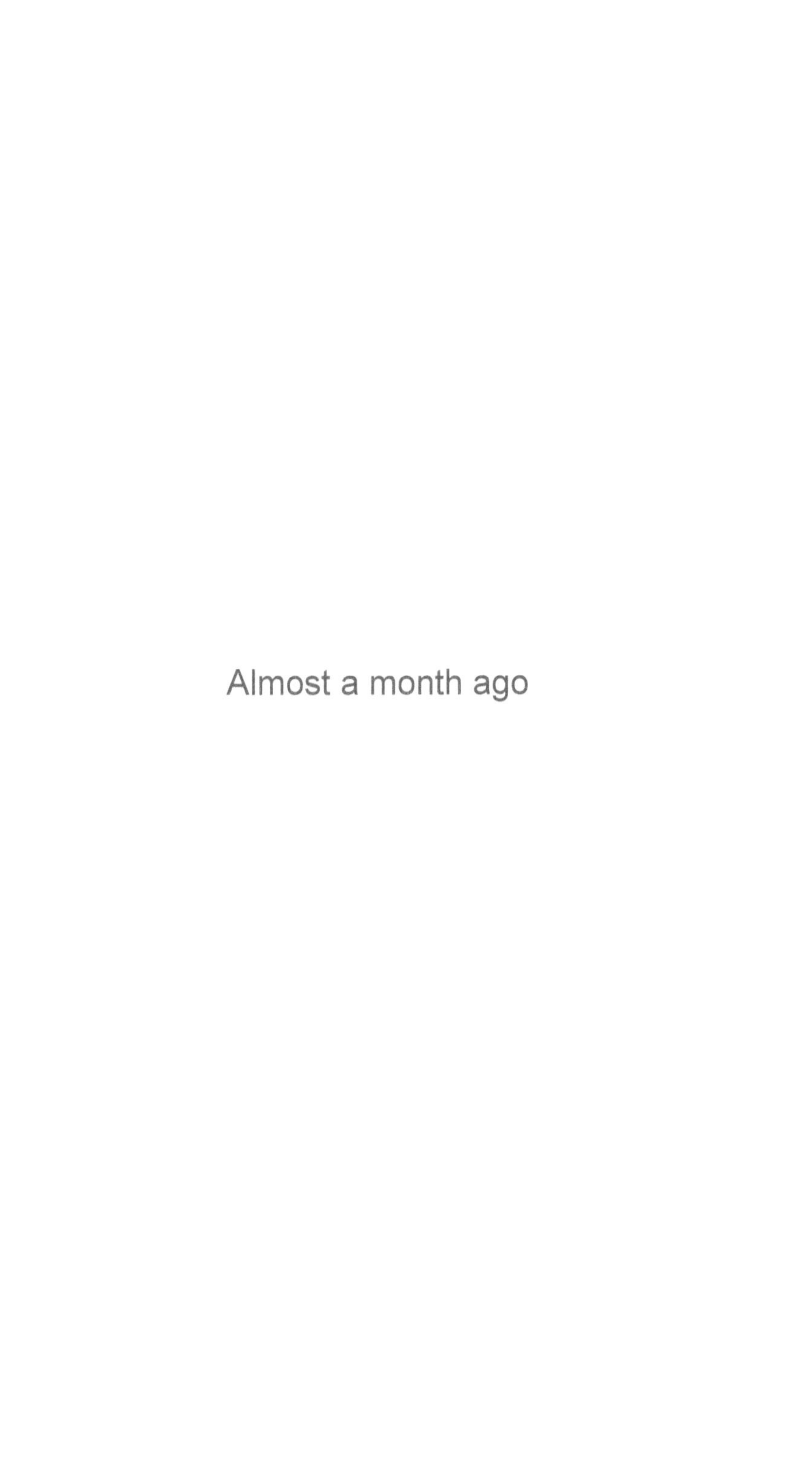
Almost a month ago

26

The late afternoon sun slanted through the warehouse's broken windows, casting fractured light across the room. Karan discussing something with his gang members.

A knock on the metal door broke the silence. Everyone was tense. Somesh straightened, his fingers tightening around the knife.

"Who's that?" he muttered, his voice low and wary.

One of the younger gang members moved hesitantly toward the door and opened it just enough to peek outside. A man stepped through, his crisp white shirt slightly wrinkled, beads of sweat dotting his forehead. He carried himself with quiet confidence, his sharp gaze taking in the room and everyone in it.

"Who the hell are you?" Somesh growled, moving closer.

The man ignored him, his attention fixed on Karan. "Your father, Krishnaiah, and I went way back," he said, his voice even. "I'm Lokesh."

Karan's eyes narrowed. "And what do you want?"

Lokesh's lips curved into a faint smile. "A deal," he said simply. "One that could change your fortunes."

The gang gathered closer, curiosity outweighing suspicion. Lokesh stepped forward, placing a stack of neatly folded papers on the desk. His movements were calm, deliberate, as if he were perfectly at ease in the tense room.

"This isn't just about money," Lokesh began, gesturing to the papers. "It's about power. The kind of power that makes the city bow to you. With the profits from this deal, you won't just survive—you'll control everything."

Somesh snorted, crossing his arms. "Sounds like a load of crap."

Lokesh's expression didn't change. "I need motorcycles—working, even old seized ones sitting in police sheds."

Karan's face remained unreadable, but there was a flicker of recognition in his eyes, "Alright," he said, his tone decisive. "We'll do it."

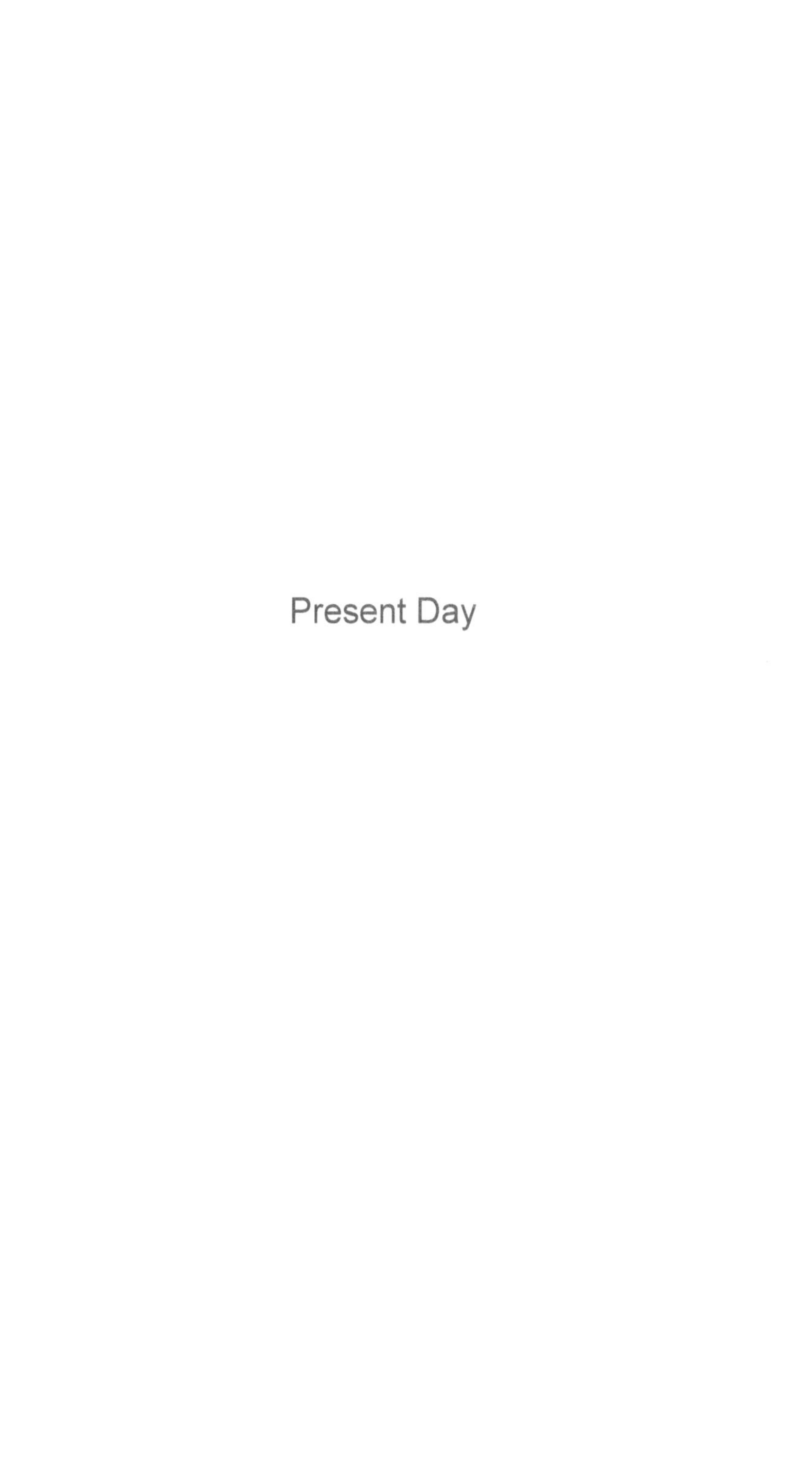
Present Day

27

The container yard loomed in darkness, towering stacks of rusted metal casting jagged shadows under the dim overhead lamps. Karan's black SUV rumbled through the eerie silence, its headlights slicing through the gloom before jerking to a halt near the central shed. Gravel crunched beneath his boots as he stepped out, his movements precise and deliberate. The air hung thick with tension, each step carrying an unspoken warning.

Inside the shed, his gang waited. Vijay and Ravi stood near the back, bruises visible even in the dim light. They avoided his gaze, shoulders hunched as if they could disappear into the shadows.

A charged silence settled as Karan entered. His footfalls echoed, tightening the atmosphere like a noose. At the battered wooden table in the center, he ran his fingers along its chipped edge—slow, deliberate. The silence stretched, heavy with anticipation.

No one dared move. Vijay swallowed hard, glancing at Ravi before stepping forward. His hands trembled slightly.

"Boss, we—"

"Shut up!" Karan's palm slammed down on the table, the crack reverberating through the shed. Everyone flinched as the tension snapped taut.

His glare pinned Vijay in place. "You thought you could handle this alone?" His voice was sharp, each word a blade. "And you didn't think to tell me about yesterday's incident?"

Vijay's mouth opened, then closed soundlessly. Ravi took a tentative step forward, voice barely above a whisper. "We didn't want to bother you, boss. It was just a small problem."

"Just a small problem?" Karan's tone turned venomous, mocking. "And now the police have our van because of your 'small problem'?"

From the corner, a slow, deliberate tapping cut through the silence. Lokesh. His fingers drummed rhythmically against the armrest of a rickety chair, the sound grating on already frayed nerves. Dressed sharply in a suit that looked absurdly out of place in the grimy setting, he exuded an air of detached superiority.

He leaned forward, eyes sharp. "If this is how your crew handles minor setbacks," he said coldly, "I'm starting to wonder if I've made a mistake."

Karan's jaw tightened, irritation flickering across his face, but his voice remained controlled. "You'll get what you're paying for. I'll fix this."

Lokesh smirked, his tone laced with disdain. "Only because I knew your father am I this patient. Don't test me."

Karan didn't flinch. His gaze shifted back to his men. "Vikram."

From the shadows, a tall, wiry figure stepped forward, silent but purposeful. Vikram's dark eyes gleamed with quiet confidence. He didn't need to speak—his presence alone commanded attention.

Karan's voice was firm. "You know what to do."

Vikram's lips curled into a slow, predatory smile.

28

The ceiling fan spun lazily, its faint hum the only sound in the otherwise silent police station. Inspector Ramana sat behind his cluttered desk, his piercing gaze fixed on Rahul and Sanjay. The fluorescent light above cast harsh shadows on the walls, amplifying the heaviness in the air.

"You boys don't understand what you've walked into," Ramana said, his tone firm but laced with caution. "Karan isn't some street-level thug. His roots go back years—back to when this city's underworld wasn't a free-for-all but a throne ruled by one name: Deva."

Rahul's fists clenched, his nails digging into his palms. The impatience bubbled to the surface, tightening his jaw. "Inspector, enough with the history lesson. We've got evidence. He's stolen motorcycles, and we've brought you proof. So what's stopping you?"

Ramana leaned back in his chair, the wooden frame creaking under his weight. He studied Rahul for a moment before letting out a slow breath, folding his arms across his chest. "Evidence is the least of your worries," he said in a quieter voice, his gaze growing distant. "Seven years ago, one gang ruled the streets—Deva's. They ran everything in this city. But when Deva was killed, Karan swore he'd rebuild what Deva left behind."

Ramana paused, his words hanging heavy in the air. "He started small—street deals, settlements. But over time, he climbed the ranks, forging ties with local politicians and criminals. His ambition is clear—he wants power, respect, and fear. But this motorcycle theft racket… that's new. We don't know why he's doing this, but it's not just about the motorcycles. There's something bigger."

Rahul's mind raced, Ramana's words painting a picture of Karan that was far more dangerous than he had imagined. He felt the weight of the inspector's words pressing on him, but the spark of defiance in his chest refused to die down.

Beside him, Sanjay shifted uncomfortably, his eyes darting between Ramana and the creaking door. The room grew tense, the weight of Ramana's revelation sinking in. The hum of the ceiling fan felt louder now, an oppressive drone cutting through the silence. Before anyone could respond, the door creaked open.

A man stepped in, his presence quiet but deliberate. Dressed in simple clothes, he walked with a calm confidence that drew immediate attention. His sharp eyes swept the room, absorbing everything, his movements unnervingly precise.

"I'm here to report a missing motorcycle," he said, his voice steady and calm.

Rahul turned to him, his eyes narrowing. Something about this man felt off, though he couldn't quite place why. His clothes were ordinary, his expression neutral—but his presence felt calculated, too composed for someone walking into a police station.

Ramana's eyes flicked to the man briefly before returning to Rahul and Sanjay, his expression unreadable.

29

The room fell quiet as Vikram took his seat across from Rahul and Sanjay at Inspector Ramana's desk. His calm, calculated demeanor seemed unsettling in the charged atmosphere.

"Last night," he said evenly, his tone devoid of emotion, "I was riding my motorcycle when two thieves came out of nowhere. They hit me, beat me up, and stole my motorcycle." His gaze shifted to Rahul and Sanjay, his eyes sharp as a blade. "Exactly like what happened to you two, no?"

Rahul clenched his fists under the table, his instincts warning him—this man wasn't just here for a missing motorcycle.

Ramana leaned forward, his fingers tapping lightly on the desk. "Interesting coincidence," he said dryly. Then, turning to an officer, he added, "Show him the van. Let's see if his motorcycle's there."

The officer gestured for Vikram to follow him. Vikram rose smoothly from his chair, his expression unreadable, and walked with deliberate steps toward the back of the station.

In the yard, the officer unlocked the van's doors, unaware of Vikram's every calculated move. As the doors creaked open, Vikram struck. His fist connected with the officer's jaw in a blur of motion, sending the man crumpling to the ground. Without hesitation, Vikram melted into the shadows, vanishing into the night.

Inside the station, the commotion reached Rahul, Sanjay, and Arjun just as they were mapping out their next steps.

Arjun's voice cut through the tension. "Now we have it—his van! Issue the warrant!"

Before they could act, a deafening roar echoed from outside. Heads snapped toward the window in time to see the van hurtling through the backyard. It smashed through parked motorcycles, leaving a trail of destruction.

30

"That's him!" Sanjay shouted, his voice laced with urgency.

Rahul didn't hesitate. "Let's go!" he barked, dragging Sanjay with him.

The sound of tires screeching against pavement tore through the dusky evening air as Vikram sped the van down the streets, bathed in the last hues of sunset blending into deepening shades of blue. The van's engine roared, echoing through the narrow alleys, while shattered glass and bent metal rattled with every sharp turn. Behind him, Rahul and Sanjay darted into action, their scooter roaring to life in pursuit.

Rahul's hands gripped Sanjay's shoulders tightly, his heart pounding as the scooter swerved to avoid debris left in the van's wake. "Faster!" he urged, his voice barely audible over the roaring engine and the distant wail of police sirens.

"I'm going as fast as this thing can handle!" Sanjay snapped, his knuckles white as he maneuvered the scooter through the chaos. Sweat beaded on his forehead, his eyes flicking between the van and the road ahead. "If we hit something, it's on you, man!"

The van's taillights flickered in the distance as it careened down an empty stretch of road. Rahul's gaze remained fixed on the vehicle, determination etched into his features. "We can't let him get away," he muttered, more to himself than to Sanjay.

The streets glowed under the first flickers of streetlights as they gave chase, the scooter weaving between parked cars and scattered trash. Vikram, aware of his pursuers, swerved violently, sending a stack of crates tumbling onto the road. Sanjay cursed under his breath, narrowly avoiding the obstacle.

"He's trying to shake us," Rahul said, his voice tense.

"No kidding," Sanjay shot back. "You'd think he'd let us catch up out of courtesy."

As the van rounded a sharp corner, Rahul's eyes widened. "Shortcut! Take the alley on the left!"

"Are you insane?" Sanjay yelled, but he followed the command, veering the scooter into a narrow, dimly lit alley. The path was littered with broken bottles and stray animals, the walls pressing in on either side.

Rahul leaned forward, his breath shallow as they emerged from the alley just ahead of the van. Vikram's eyes narrowed as he spotted them, his grip tightening on the wheel. The van swerved, aiming to clip the scooter.

"Hold on!" Sanjay shouted, jerking the handlebars to avoid the collision. The scooter tipped dangerously but regained balance as it sped alongside the van.

Rahul's heart raced as he saw his chance. "Get closer!" he yelled.

"Are you kidding me?" Sanjay's voice cracked with panic. "You're not serious…"

"Closer!" Rahul's voice was steel. He adjusted his position, his muscles coiling like a spring.

With a deep breath, Rahul leapt from the scooter onto the side of the van. His hands scrambled for a grip on the battered metal, the wind tearing at his clothes as the van swayed. His feet found a precarious foothold on the wheel well, his body pressed flat against the side.

"Rahul!" Sanjay's voice faded behind him as the scooter fell back, its engine sputtering.

Inside the van, Vikram's focus wavered. He glanced in the side mirror, his jaw tightening as he saw Rahul clinging to the side. With a snarl, he swerved violently, trying to shake him off.

Rahul gritted his teeth, his fingers screaming in protest as the van bucked beneath him. He edged closer to the driver's door, his gaze locked on Vikram. With a burst of effort, he grabbed the door handle and yanked it open.

The wind howled as the door swung wide. Vikram's hand shot out, grabbing at Rahul's wrist. The two men struggled, the confined space amplifying every movement. Vikram's strength was formidable, but Rahul's resolve was unyielding.

"You've messed with the wrong people," Rahul growled, his voice raw.

Vikram's response was a sharp elbow to Rahul's ribs. Pain lanced through him, but he refused to let go. His free hand fumbled beneath the driver's seat, fingers closing around a wrench. With all his strength, he swung it at Vikram's arm.

The impact was brutal. Vikram yelped, his grip loosening. Rahul seized the opportunity, pulling himself into the van. The two men grappled, their movements a blur of fists and elbows. The van swerved wildly, tires screeching as it veered off the road.

Ahead, a utility pole loomed. Rahul's eyes widened. "Jump!" he shouted, shoving Vikram away as he threw himself out of the van.

He hit the ground hard, pain exploding through his body as he rolled to a stop. Behind him, the van collided with the pole in a deafening crash, flames erupting as the engine exploded. Heat washed over Rahul, the twilight sky flashing bright with an explosion's glow.

Groaning, Rahul pushed himself onto his elbows, his vision swimming. In the distance, a figure staggered toward him. Vikram's face was a mask of fury, his steps unsteady but purposeful.

Rahul's limbs felt like lead, his body refusing to move. He braced himself for the worst when the roar of an engine cut through the chaos. Sanjay appeared on the scooter, his expression a mix of panic and determination.

"Move!" Sanjay shouted.

The scooter slammed into Vikram, sending him sprawling onto the pavement. Sanjay skidded to a stop, the scooter toppling over as he jumped off.

He hurried to Rahul's side, offering a hand. "Get up, man. We're not done yet."

Rahul took the hand, his grip weak but steady. As police sirens grew louder in the distance, the two friends stood together, the wreckage of the van burning behind them. For a brief moment, they exchanged a glance—a silent acknowledgment that this was far from over.

31

The remnants of chaos lingered in the air—burnt rubber, the metallic tang of gasoline, and the faint acrid smell of smoke. Rahul and Sanjay stood at the edge of the wreckage, their bodies stiff with exhaustion. Sirens wailed in the background as the police swarmed the scene, their voices sharp and urgent as they barked orders.

Rahul's gaze followed the officers as they wrestled Vikram into the back of the police van. His mind was a storm, fragments of the chase replaying in sharp, jagged flashes. The crunch of metal, the blinding firelight, the sound of Vikram's boots hitting the pavement—it was all too vivid. But now, there was silence. A heavy, suffocating silence that weighed on his chest.

"What now?" Sanjay's voice broke through, low and uncertain. He adjusted the strap of his bag, his eyes darting nervously between the officers and the smoldering van. "Do we just… leave?"

Rahul's jaw tightened. His hands ached, the cuts on his palms stinging with every pulse of his heartbeat. But what else could they do? The police had taken control of the scene, their presence a stark reminder of how little power Rahul and Sanjay truly had.

Without answering, Rahul turned on his heel, his steps heavy as he walked away from the wreckage. Sanjay hesitated but followed, casting one last glance at the police van before they disappeared into the growing crowd.

From the shadows of a nearby rooftop, Karan watched the scene unfold. His face was obscured by the black scarf wrapped tightly around his mouth and nose, leaving only his cold, calculating eyes visible. He observed the chaos with a detached calm, noting every movement, every misstep of the officers as they fumbled to secure the area.

"Enough," Karan muttered under his breath, his voice muffled by the scarf. His gloved hand tightened around the handlebar of his motorcycle. The decision was made in an instant.

The engine roared to life as Karan sped toward the scene, weaving through the narrow alleys that flanked the wreckage. The sound of his arrival was drowned out by the cacophony of sirens and shouted commands. He dismounted swiftly, moving with the kind of precision that spoke of years spent in the shadows.

32

Karan's sharp eyes scanned the area. The officers were distracted, their attention split between the crowd and the evidence they were cataloging. He moved like a phantom, closing the distance to the van without a single wasted motion.

Karan didn't speak. Instead, he pulled a handgun from his jacket, its dark finish gleaming under the flickering streetlight. The shot rang out, shattering the cuffs around Vikram's wrists. The sound was swallowed by the commotion outside, barely registering among the shouts and sirens.

Karan reached into his jacket again, this time retrieving a small, cylindrical object. Vikram's eyes widened as realization dawned.

"Smoke grenade," Karan said, his voice low but commanding. "Stay close."

He pulled the pin and tossed the grenade to the ground. It erupted in a plume of thick, black smoke, spreading rapidly and swallowing the area in darkness. The acrid scent stung their nostrils, but neither flinched. Vikram pushed himself to his feet, his movements sluggish but determined.

The two vanished into the smoke, their silhouettes blending into the swirling chaos. Shouts erupted from the officers as they scrambled to regain control, their flashlights cutting through the haze with little success.

33

The apartment sat in heavy silence, broken only by the slow creak of the fan overhead. Rahul leaned against the wall near the door, arms crossed, the weight of the evening pressing down on him like a vice. His gaze stayed fixed on the floor, his mind a tangle of half-formed plans and dead-end thoughts.

From the living room, his mother's voice cut through the stillness.

"Rahul, come here."

He turned, finding her seated on the worn couch, the dim street light outside casting uneven shadows across her face. Worry lined her features, deepened by the flickering glow. She gestured for him to sit, but he stayed where he was, his posture rigid.

"Where's your motorcycle?" she asked, her voice steady but laced with something softer, something that made his chest tighten. "You've been gone all day."

His fingers curled into fists at his sides. He couldn't tell her. Not now.

"It's… being repaired," he muttered, the words brittle in his mouth.

A lump lodged in his throat, but he forced it down and met her eyes.

"I'll be back soon, Ma," he said, sidestepping her words.

He turned toward the door, but her voice pulled him back.

"Rahul." It was a plea now, strained and breaking.

"I'll be back," he repeated, firmer this time, and stepped out into the night.

Sanjay was waiting by his scooter at the curb, the engine humming softly. He glanced up as Rahul approached, his face a mix of concern and quiet understanding.

"Ready?"

Rahul climbed onto the back. "Let's go."

They rode in silence, the city stretching dark and endless around them. The hum of the scooter filled the space between them, but Rahul barely noticed. His thoughts churned—Karan, the gang, the risks ahead. The night air bit at his skin, but he didn't feel it.

He had already made his choice.

34

The grand gates of Anwar's mansion loomed ahead, their black iron bars gleaming under the pale glow of the streetlights. Two guards stood at attention, their silhouettes sharp against the sprawling property beyond. As the scooter rolled to a stop, Rahul slid off, his resolve hardening as he approached the intercom.

Sanjay hovered a step behind, his movements uncharacteristically hesitant. "You sure about this?" he murmured, his voice barely audible.

Rahul ignored him, pressing the buzzer firmly. A faint crackle followed, then a voice. "Who is it?"

"Rahul," he said simply. "Tell Anwar I need to see him."

The guard's eyes narrowed as he stepped closer, his hand hovering near the holster at his hip. "Do you have an appointment?"

"No," Rahul replied, his tone steady. "But he'll want to hear what I have to say."

The guard studied him for a long moment before muttering into a device clipped to his collar. After a tense pause, the gates creaked open, the sound echoing in the stillness. Rahul and Sanjay exchanged a brief glance before stepping inside.

The mansion was a stark contrast to the chaos Rahul had been steeped in for days. Chandeliers glimmered overhead, casting soft light on the polished floors and ornate furnishings. The air smelled faintly of cedar and something floral, a scent that felt oddly out of place given the circumstances.

The guards led them to a study near the back of the house. Anwar sat behind a mahogany desk, a crystal glass in his hand. He glanced up as they entered, his sharp eyes narrowing slightly.

"Rahul?" he said, his tone clipped. "What are you doing here at this hour?"

Rahul stepped forward, ignoring the plush chair Anwar gestured toward. "I need your help."

Anwar leaned back in his chair, setting the glass down with a soft clink. "Help?" he echoed, his expression unreadable. "And what kind of help do you think I can offer?"

Rahul launched into his explanation without preamble. The stolen motorcycle. Karan. The escalating danger. He spoke quickly, his words laced with urgency. When he finished, the room fell silent, the weight of his story hanging heavily in the air.

Anwar's expression darkened, his fingers steepling beneath his chin. "You've gotten yourself into something dangerous, Rahul. Do you have any idea who you're up against?"

Rahul met his gaze, unflinching. "I don't have a choice. The police won't help, and I can't do this alone. You know, you owed my father your life. It's time to make good on that."

The mention of Rahul's father made Anwar's jaw tighten. His gaze dropped to the desk, a flicker of something unreadable passing through his eyes.

"Your father didn't hesitate that day. He risked everything to save me. And now, in a way, that's why you're standing here." He exhaled sharply. "Maybe this is fate's way of balancing the scales."

He reached for his phone, dialing with deliberate precision. "Fine," he said, his tone brisk. "I'll help. But understand this—once you step into this world, there's no turning back."

Rahul nodded, his chest tightening. "I know."

Anwar studied him for a moment before speaking into the phone. His words were clipped, efficient. When he hung up, his gaze lingered on Rahul.

"This isn't just about your father anymore. This is about you."

Rahul held his ground, the weight of Anwar's words settling in his chest. "I'll handle it," he said quietly.

Anwar sighed, leaning back in his chair. "You'd better."

35

The grand gates of Anwar's mansion loomed ahead, their black iron bars gleaming under the pale streetlights. Two guards stood at attention, their silhouettes sharp against the sprawling estate beyond. As the scooter rolled to a stop, Rahul swung off, exhaling slowly before striding toward the intercom.

Sanjay lingered a step behind, his usual bravado noticeably absent. "You sure about this?" he murmured.

Rahul didn't answer. He pressed the buzzer firmly. A faint crackle followed before a voice came through. "Who is it?"

"Rahul," he said simply. "Tell Anwar I need to see him."

One of the guards stepped forward, his gaze sharp. "Do you have an appointment?"

"No," Rahul replied, his voice even. "But he'll want to hear what I have to say."

The guard studied him for a moment before muttering into his earpiece. After a tense pause, the gates groaned open. Rahul and Sanjay exchanged a glance before stepping inside.

The mansion was a stark contrast to the chaos Rahul had been steeped in for days. Chandeliers cast a soft glow over polished floors, the scent of cedar and something floral lingering in the air. It was unsettlingly calm.

They were led through a corridor to a study near the back. Anwar sat behind a mahogany desk, a crystal glass in his hand. He glanced up as they entered, his sharp eyes narrowing slightly.

"Rahul," he said, his tone clipped. "This is unexpected."

Rahul stepped forward, ignoring the plush chair Anwar gestured toward. "I need your help."

Anwar leaned back, setting his glass down with a quiet clink. "Help?" he echoed. "And what exactly do you expect me to do?"

Rahul launched into his explanation. The stolen motorcycle. Karan. The danger closing in. He spoke quickly, urgency threading through his words. When he finished, the room settled into a heavy silence.

Anwar steepled his fingers beneath his chin. "You've gotten yourself into something dangerous, Rahul. Do you even understand who you're dealing with?"

Rahul held his gaze. "I don't have a choice. The police won't help, and I can't do this alone." He hesitated before adding, "You owe my father your life. It's time to settle that debt."

A flicker of something unreadable passed through Anwar's eyes. His jaw tightened as he glanced down at his desk.

"Your father didn't hesitate that day," he said finally. "Risked everything to save me." He exhaled sharply. "Maybe this is fate's way of balancing the scales."

He reached for his phone, dialing with deliberate precision. "Fine," he said. "I'll help."

Rahul hesitated, then spoke with quiet resolve. "I need men—people who aren't afraid to fight back."

"If we're going to do this, we need backup."

Anwar exhaled slowly, measuring Rahul with a long stare. The silence stretched before he finally gave a small, decisive nod. "Alright. I'll send you two of my best. But understand this—once you're in, it doesn't end until one side falls."

Rahul's pulse pounded in his ears, but he didn't flinch. "I'm ready."

36

The streets lay eerily silent as Rahul, Sanjay, and the two men Anwar had sent made their way to Swamy's mechanic shop. The dim yellow glow of the streetlights stretched their shadows long across the cracked pavement, each footstep echoing in the stillness.

Rahul's chest tightened as they neared the door. The sharp scent of grease and oil hung in the air, a stark contrast to the tension coursing through him. He pushed the door open, its creak slicing through the quiet like a warning.

Inside, Swamy lounged in a battered chair, chewing paan. His stained fingers tapped idly against the armrest as his sharp eyes landed on the group. A slow smirk tugged at his lips.

"Well, well," he drawled, his tone thick with mockery. "The kid brings backup now."

Rahul ignored the jab and stepped forward. The two men flanked him, their silence speaking louder than words. Around the shop, workers edged back, the clink of tools against concrete the only sound.

"I'm not here to waste time," Rahul said, his voice even. "I need information about Karan."

Swamy chuckled, leaning back. "Karan, huh? You're braver than I thought, kid. Or just dumber."

Rahul's fists tightened at his sides, but his voice stayed calm. "You know something, and you're going to tell me."

Swamy's smirk faltered—just slightly. His gaze flicked to the men behind Rahul. After a long pause, he sighed.

"Fine. Deva's gang fell apart years ago. Karan picked up the pieces, but it's not the same. If you really want answers, there's only one man who knows the whole story—Somesh. He was close to Deva before everything crumbled. Now he works for Karan."

"Where is he?" Rahul asked.

Swamy hesitated before waving a lazy hand. "Near the railway station, by the edge of the market. That's all I know."

Rahul gave a small nod, his expression unreadable as he turned to leave. He had barely reached the door when Swamy's voice stopped him.

"Kid," he said, his tone carrying a hint of something—warning, maybe amusement. "Brave or stupid… hard to tell."

Rahul didn't answer. The night air hit him like a slap as he stepped outside, the cold clearing his mind. Each step toward the railway station felt heavier, the path ahead thick with uncertainty. As they neared Somesh's dilapidated house, Rahul steeled himself for whatever came next.

37

Rahul, Sanjay, and the two hired men from Anwar stood outside Somesh's dilapidated house near the railway station. The faint hum of a passing train in the distance added to the tension. The house, with its peeling paint and rusted iron bars, was a stark contrast to the significance of its occupant—a man who held the answers Rahul desperately needed. The faint glow of a television flickered through the window, signaling Somesh's presence.

Rahul raised a hand, signaling silence, then knocked firmly on the door. There was a pause, then the door creaked open just a crack. Somesh's wary eyes appeared, scanning the group. His gaze lingered on the hired men, their intimidating presence making him visibly uneasy, before shifting to Rahul

"What do you want?" Somesh asked, his voice laced with caution.

Rahul stepped forward, his tone steady and firm. "We're here about Karan. Swamy said you'd know where to find him."

Somesh stiffened, his hand tightening on the door. "I don't know what you're talking about. Now get lost."

Rahul's voice didn't waver. "We're not leaving until you talk."

Somesh began to close the door, but one of the hired men blocked it with his foot. The man leaned in, his tone low and menacing. "You can talk now, or we'll make this unpleasant."

Somesh's eyes darted around in panic, weighing his options. Then, in a desperate move, he shoved Rahul aside and bolted through a side door.

"After him!" Rahul shouted, sprinting after Somesh without hesitation.

The chase erupted through narrow alleys and dimly lit streets, a chaotic tangle of footsteps echoing in the night. The hired men split up, moving quickly to flank Somesh. Rahul kept up, his determination outweighing exhaustion, while Sanjay lagged behind, muttering curses as he stumbled over uneven ground.

Somesh darted toward the railway tracks, trying to disappear into the shadows of a slow-moving train. But one of the hired men was faster. He lunged, grabbing Somesh by the collar and slamming him hard against a chain-link fence.

"Enough running," the man growled, holding him firmly in place.

Somesh stood cornered, breathing heavily. Sanjay stepped forward, his hands trembling as he gripped the prop gun tighter than he needed to. His voice cracked slightly, but the determination was clear. "Talk!" he shouted, pointing the prop gun. The weapon's presence alone froze Somesh, who raised his hands in surrender, his eyes darting between the hired men and Rahul.

38

"Alright! I'll talk! Just… don't do anything stupid!" Somesh's words spilled out, his voice shaking. He glanced nervously at the prop gun, clearly unaware of its harmlessness.

"Where's Karan and the stolen motorcycles?" Rahul's voice was steady, his steps deliberate as he moved closer. His shadow fell over Somesh, who shrank back against the fence.

Somesh hesitated, licking his lips nervously. "He's… he's at a container yard near the port. That's his base. That's where the motorcycles are." Sanjay subtly shifted his phone, the camera's red recording light glinting faintly as he captured every word."

Sanjay stepped forward, his frustration boiling over. "What's he doing with them? What's the point of stealing so many motorcycles?"

Somesh hesitated again, glancing nervously at the men standing like silent statues behind Rahul. Sanjay gave Rahul a brief nod, the phone still recording. "It's political," Somesh muttered, almost as if admitting it hurt him, his voice quieter now. "It's MLA Ravi Shetty, from Mangalore. He's up for re-election. He's been promising free motorcycles to the youth if they vote for him—and if their families vote, too. Karan's just a middleman, managing the supply here. They've been collecting motorcycles from across states."

"You're ruining lives for someone's greed," Rahul said, stepping back and exhaling sharply. "We've got what we need. Get out of here."

Somesh didn't wait to be told twice. He stumbled away, rubbing his bruised arms. As he reached the tracks, he patted his pocket instinctively, his hand freezing when he realized his phone was missing. He glanced back toward Rahul and the others, but they were already gone, swallowed by the night. Panic filled his eyes as he frantically searched the ground, knowing he couldn't warn Karan without it.

Rahul and Sanjay walked briskly toward the container yard, the hired men trailing closely. The city's lights grew dimmer as they approached the industrial zone. Rahul pulled out his phone and dialed Inspector Ramana, his voice sharp and direct.

"We found out what's happening," Rahul said. "Karan's stealing motorcycles for Ravi Shetty's election campaign. He's promising free motorcycles to secure votes."

Beside him, Sanjay pulled up his phone and played the video recording of Somesh's confession, the dim light catching the incriminating footage as Somesh's words echoed from the device.

On the other end, Ramana's tone was grave. "This is serious. Send me the recording."

Sanjay forwarded the file quickly. There was a pause before Ramana spoke again. "I've got it. This is enough to start the process. I'll issue warrants. But listen, you've done enough. Let us handle it from here. This is dangerous."

Rahul exchanged a look with Sanjay, who shook his head slightly. Rahul didn't respond to Ramana's advice. Instead, he ended the call and slipped the phone into his pocket.

39

The container yard buzzed with motion and sound. Trucks roared to life, their engines rumbling as containers were hoisted and loaded. The harsh glare of floodlights cast long, jagged shadows over the stacks of metal containers. Rahul crouched behind a stack of crates with Sanjay and the two hired men from Anwar, his eyes scanning the chaotic operation.

"They're moving the motorcycles," Rahul muttered, his jaw tightening. He glanced at the hired men, their faces grim and ready. "We don't have time. Let's move."

Without waiting for an answer, he motioned for them to follow. They darted forward, weaving through the shadows. Rocks clattered against glass, shattering the windshields of parked trucks. The drivers scrambled out, shouting in confusion, and chaos spread like wildfire.

Goons poured out of the containers, some armed with rods, others barehanded but itching for a fight. The two hired men met the first wave head-on, fists flying, while Rahul and Sanjay slipped deeper into the labyrinth of containers.

"Check every container!" Rahul shouted, his voice cutting through the noise. He grabbed a rusted lever lying nearby and jammed it into the lock of the nearest container. With a grunt, he wrenched the door open, revealing stacks of motorcycles inside, neatly lined like captured soldiers.

Sanjay darted to another container, his hands trembling as he pried it open. Rows of motorcycles gleamed under the dim light, their chrome surfaces reflecting the flickering yard lights. But none of them were Rahul's.

Inside another container, Sanjay's phone buzzed loudly, startling him. He fumbled for it, his hands shaking. Arjun's name flashed on the screen.

"Where are you? What's going on? The inspector sent backup!" Arjun's voice was sharp, almost frantic.

"I'm inside a container yard," Sanjay hissed, his words rushed. "I found the motorcycles. I'll send the location. Just get here fast."

He hung up before Arjun could protest.

Then he saw it. The motorcycle.

40

His heart raced as he stepped closer. It was unmistakable—the scratches on the fuel tank, the small dent on the side. Relief surged through him, but only for a moment. The ignition was empty.

"No keys," he muttered, his voice trembling with frustration. He stepped out of the container, shouting, "Rahul! I found your motorcycle, but there are no keys!"

Rahul was in the thick of it. A goon lunged at him with a rod, but Rahul ducked, twisting his body to deliver a sharp punch to the man's ribs. Another attacker rushed him, but one of the hired men intercepted, slamming the goon to the ground with a bone-crunching thud.

Amidst the chaos, Sanjay's voice carried over the noise. "Rahul! No keys!"

Rahul's head snapped toward the sound. He spotted Sanjay near the container, his silhouette frantic.

Reaching into his pocket, Rahul's fingers brushed against the familiar metal shape. The spare keys.

Without hesitation, he pulled them out and flung them toward Sanjay. The keys sailed through the air, glinting under the yard lights before disappearing into the shadows between rows of motorcycles.

"No!" Sanjay shouted, dropping to his knees. He scrambled between the motorcycles, his hands frantically searching the ground. The hired men, preoccupied with holding off the advancing goons, couldn't help.

Rahul took a deep breath, his mind racing. He turned to the nearest goon, grabbing the rod from his hands and shoving him aside. "Hold them off!" he shouted to the hired men before sprinting toward Sanjay.

Sanjay's hands brushed against gravel, oil stains, and discarded tools, but the keys were nowhere in sight. "I can't find them!" he yelled, his voice desperate.

Rahul reached him, dropping to his knees beside him. His sharp eyes scanned the ground, darting between the motorcycles. "Focus," he said, his tone calm but firm. "We'll find them."

Then, in the faint light beneath a motorcycle, Rahul saw a glint of silver. "There!" He pointed, reaching under the motorcycle and pulling out the keys. Relief flooded his face as he handed them to Sanjay. "Go. Start it."

Sanjay grabbed the keys, his hands trembling as he sprinted toward the motorcycle. Sliding onto the seat, he jammed the key into the ignition and twisted. The engine roared to life, its sound cutting through the night like a victory cry.

41

The commotion drew attention. A voice rang out, sharp and angry. "Hey! They're taking the motorcycle! Stop them!"

Heads turned, and a wave of goons surged toward them. Sanjay twisted the throttle, the motorcycle growling like a caged beast. "Get on, Rahul!" he yelled, his voice edged with panic.

Rahul dashed toward him, dodging the chaos of the yard. He leapt onto the motorcycle, his hands gripping the handlebars as it lurched forward. But just as he twisted the throttle, a metallic clang echoed from above. His eyes darted upward.

A shadow moved, then dropped down with deadly precision.

Karan.

He landed with a thud, rising slowly, his imposing figure illuminated by the flickering yard lights. His smirk was razor-sharp, his eyes locked onto Rahul with cold intensity.

"Not so fast," Karan said, his voice calm but menacing.

42

Rahul's jaw clenched. Without a second's hesitation, he revved the engine, the motorcycle roaring as it surged forward. Dust kicked up behind the tires as he aimed the motorcycle straight at Karan.

But Karan didn't flinch. As the motorcycle hurtled toward him, he sidestepped with unnerving agility, the rush of air brushing past him. His hand shot out, grabbing Rahul by the collar. With a brutal yank, Rahul was ripped off the motorcycle, his body crashing to the ground with a sickening thud.

The motorcycle skidded, its wheels screeching as it toppled onto its side, sliding a few feet before coming to a stop. Sanjay barely held on, his grip on the handlebars saving him from being thrown off.

Rahul groaned, pain radiating through his body as he rolled onto his side. He pushed himself up, his vision spinning. Karan stood over him, towering and unshaken, his smirk replaced with a hardened glare.

"Did you really think you could escape from me?" Karan sneered, his voice venomous.

Rahul staggered to his feet, wiping blood from the corner of his mouth. His fists clenched as he steadied himself.

Behind them, Sanjay struggled to right the fallen motorcycle. His hands shook as he tried to lift it, but his gaze kept darting back to Rahul. "Rahul! " he yelled, desperation creeping into his voice.

Rahul didn't respond. His eyes never left Karan, his mind racing. Around them, the remaining goons began to close in, forming a loose circle. Their shouts and jeers rang out, but Rahul's focus was razor-sharp, honed in on the man standing before him.

"You've caused enough trouble," Karan said, stepping closer. "Now, I'll finish this myself."

Rahul took a deep breath, his muscles coiled like a spring.

Rahul and Sanjay stood frozen for a split second as Karan stepped closer. The yard lights flickered, illuminating his sharp, calculated movements. He adjusted the beanie and sunglasses perched on his face, his calm exterior masking the simmering storm beneath.

Rahul clenched his fists, his knuckles white as he sized up the imposing figure before him. His muscles ached, but he refused to back down.

43

The screech of an auto-rickshaw's abrupt stop cut through the muffled cacophony of the container yard. Dust swirled beneath the flickering street lights as the vehicle jerked to a halt. Arjun stepped out, his pulse quickening as his eyes darted over the scene. Sanjay's battered scooter leans precariously against the fence, half-concealed by shadows.

Something was wrong. A knot formed in Arjun's stomach. He yanked his phone from his pocket, his hands trembling slightly as he dialed.

"Inspector Ramana," he said, keeping his voice low but tense. "Where are you?"

"On the way," Ramana's reply was curt, laced with urgency. "Listen to me, Arjun—don't engage. Wait for backup."

Before Arjun could argue, the line went dead. He stared at the phone for a moment before shoving it back into his pocket. The thought of waiting made his chest tighten. Rahul and Sanjay were inside, and every second felt like sand slipping through an hourglass. He couldn't stand still.

The auto driver watched him warily as Arjun thrust a few crumpled bills into his hand. "Keep the change," he muttered before turning toward the gates. His steps were quick but deliberate, his resolve hardening with every stride. Shadows pooled in the corners of the yard, the air thick with an unsettling tension that seemed to hang over the entire area.

Further ahead, Arjun caught a glimpse of Sanjay scrambling up the ladder of a crane, his movements frantic. What the hell is he doing? Arjun thought, his mind racing. The scene was chaotic, but he couldn't afford to hesitate.

He pressed himself against the cool metal of a container, his breathing shallow. He had to act fast, but his thoughts tangled as he tried to piece together a plan. The inspector's warning echoed in his ears, but the urgency of the moment drowned it out. Rahul and Sanjay needed him, and there was no time to wait.

44

In the scuffle, Karan's beanie slipped off, fluttering to the ground. The sunglasses followed, hitting the dirt with a sharp crack. The lens shattered, sending tiny shards flying. One shard grazed Karan's hand, leaving a thin but visible cut that trickled with blood.

The change in Karan's demeanor was immediate. His smirk vanished, replaced by a storm of fury. He stared at the broken sunglasses, his chest rising and falling with short, furious breaths. His hand clenched into a fist, the blood from the cut dripping onto the ground.

Sanjay's eyes darted around frantically. The circle of goons was tightening, their aggressive energy growing as they sensed the impending fight. He knew Rahul wouldn't back down, but Karan was no ordinary opponent. He had to find a way to shift the odds.

His gaze landed on a crane towering over the yard, its rusted arm stretched out like a skeletal hand. An idea sparked. Without thinking twice, he broke into a run, weaving through the maze of containers toward the crane. His breath came in sharp bursts as he reached the base of the machine. A battered ladder led up to the operator's cabin.

"Please work, please work," Sanjay muttered under his breath as he climbed. His palms were slick with sweat, slipping slightly on the rungs. He reached the cabin, fumbling with the controls. The panel was old, the buttons faded and unmarked, but he didn't care. He slammed his hand down, and the crane roared to life, its groan loud enough to cut through the yard's noise.

The sudden sound drew attention. Heads turned, and one of the goons shouted, "What's he doing up there?! Stop him!"

Arjun seized the moment. While the goons' focus shifted to Sanjay, he darted forward, his steps silent but quick. He grabbed a length of pipe lying on the ground, gripping it tightly as he moved toward the circle.

Rahul didn't glance away from Karan, even as the crane roared to life behind him. "This ends here," he said, his voice low but firm.

Karan's lips curled into a sneer. "You're out of your depth, kid. This isn't your fight."

Rahul's eyes hardened. "It became my fight the moment you stole from me—and from all those people you've hurt."

Karan lunged suddenly, his movements swift and forceful. Rahul sidestepped, narrowly avoiding the blow, and retaliated with a punch to Karan's ribs. The crowd of goons erupted into shouts as the fight began, their cheers and jeers blending into a cacophony.

Above them, Sanjay grinned, his characteristic sarcasm bubbling to the surface even in the chaos. "Bet you didn't expect me to be the guy operating heavy machinery, huh?" he muttered to himself. His fingers fumbled over the unfamiliar controls, each button pressed tentative and unsure. The crane jerked into motion with a loud groan, swinging the claw over the containers in a wild, almost uncoordinated arc. "This is exactly how video games help in real life," he added dryly, smirking as the goons scrambled to avoid the erratic movements. "I'm an artist," he muttered, maneuvering the claw to lift a container off a truck. The massive steel box hung suspended in the air, swaying slightly.

"Rahul!" Sanjay shouted from the cabin, his voice barely audible over the noise. "I'm clearing the way! Get ready!"

Arjun burst into the circle just as Rahul landed another hit on Karan. The pipe in Arjun's hands swung hard, striking one of the goons who had moved in to interfere. The man crumpled with a grunt, and Arjun stepped beside Rahul.

"I told you not to go alone," Arjun said breathlessly, his eyes scanning the chaos.

Rahul smirked, wiping the sweat from his brow. "Good timing."

Karan, now furious, glared at both of them. "You think you can beat me? This is my territory."

The crane's claw swung again, slamming into a stack of motorcycles. Metal crashed against metal as the motorcycles toppled, scattering across the ground. The goons hesitated, some stepping back as the crane continued its assault.

Rahul's grip on the situation tightened. The tide was turning, but the fight wasn't over yet.

45

Anwar's two hired men fought fiercely, exchanging blows with the gang of goons. Metal pipes clashed against fists, and the sounds of grunts and shouts echoed through the night. Dust filled the air as the chaos of the battle spilled into every corner of the container yard.

In the center of it all, Rahul and Karan were locked in a ferocious battle. They circled each other like predators, their eyes burning with resolve. Karan struck first, a swift jab to Rahul's side, but Rahul countered with a powerful punch that landed squarely on Karan's jaw. The sharp impact sent a dull ache through Rahul's fist, but he didn't flinch.

Their movements were relentless, a clash of strength against speed. Rahul's punches carried weight, each strike aimed to end the fight, but Karan's agility allowed him to slip away, retaliating with sharp, precise hits. The two were evenly matched, their raw determination fueling each brutal exchange.

Rahul's breath came in short bursts, his muscles aching with each swing. He didn't let the exhaustion show, though he could feel it creeping in. Karan's quick reflexes began to give him an edge. He ducked under Rahul's next punch and delivered a sharp kick to his ribs, sending Rahul stumbling back. Pain radiated through Rahul's side, but he gritted his teeth, refusing to give Karan the satisfaction of seeing him falter.

Before Rahul could recover, Karan closed the distance, raising his fist for a crushing blow. Suddenly, a blur of motion interrupted. Arjun charged forward with a guttural yell, tackling Karan with all his weight. The impact sent both men tumbling to the ground, rolling across the dirt.

Karan's figure moved swiftly, his boots finding purchase on the steel rungs of the container's side. His climb was purposeful, each motion driven by his relentless determination to reach Sanjay at the top. The flickering yard lights cast his shadow long and jagged against the container, adding an eerie edge to his ascent.

Rahul spotted him from below, his chest tightening at the sight. He didn't hesitate. Without a word, he grabbed the nearest ladder rung, his muscles straining as he pulled himself upward. The chaotic shouts and metallic clangs from the yard faded into the background as his focus sharpened on one thing—stopping Karan.

As Rahul hauled himself onto the top of the container, his breath came in sharp bursts. Karan was already there, standing tall, his stance confident as he turned to face Rahul. Their eyes locked, the charged silence between them broken only by the groaning crane suspending the container high above the ground.

For a moment, neither moved. The tension crackled in the air, a storm waiting to break.

46

Rahul's fists clenched, his jaw tightening. He didn't wait for Karan to make the first move. With a burst of energy, he charged forward, his footsteps pounding against the steel as he closed the distance. His fist arced through the air, aiming straight for Karan.

Karan sneered, his fists tightening. "You should've stayed down," he spat.

Rahul wiped the blood from his lip, his grin defiant. "I'll stay down when this is over."

Karan lunged first, throwing a powerful punch aimed at Rahul's face. Rahul sidestepped with agility, the wind of the missed punch brushing past his cheek. Without hesitation, Rahul countered, driving a jab into Karan's ribs. The force of the blow sent a sharp grunt from Karan, but it wasn't enough to stop him.

With a quick pivot, Karan retaliated, his fist connecting with Rahul's jaw. The impact sent Rahul stumbling back, his boots skidding against the container's surface. Karan smirked, his confidence unshaken. "You're outmatched," he taunted, his voice sharp and cutting.

Rahul steadied himself, blood dripping from the corner of his mouth. He spit to the side, his eyes blazing. "We'll see about that."

Fueled by the sting of the blow and his unwavering resolve, Rahul surged forward, tackling Karan with all his strength. The impact drove Karan to the steel floor of the container, and the two men grappled fiercely. Their bodies rolled dangerously close to the edge, the drop below threatening to swallow them both.

Karan snarled, twisting to throw Rahul off, but Rahul's legs locked around Karan's torso like a vice. His arms clung tightly to Karan, refusing to let go.

"You think this is enough?" Karan hissed, his voice strained as he struggled against Rahul's grip.

Rahul's voice was low but firm, his grip unyielding. "This ends here, Karan. No more motorcycles. No more victims. No more lies."

The container swayed again, the crane groaning under the shifting weight. Below them, the flashing red and blue lights of the police lit up the yard.

Officers shouted commands, clearing out the last remnants of Karan's operation.

But above it all, atop the swaying steel, the final confrontation raged on.

"Give it up, man!" Rahul hissed through gritted teeth, his muscles straining as he held Karan in a vice-like grip. Sweat dripped down his brow, his chest heaving from the exertion.

Karan's gaze darted downward for a brief second. The dizzying height below them—the ground far out of reach—made him hesitate. But only for a moment. His lips curled into a sneer, his fury undiminished.

"Never!" Karan spat, his voice laced with venom.

Before Rahul could respond, the container jerked violently, the crane halting with a sudden lurch. The abrupt motion sent a shockwave through both men, making them stumble. For a split second, the fight froze, their balance precarious as the steel beneath them groaned under the shifting weight.

Karan recovered first. Seizing the moment, he pushed against Rahul with all his strength, his palms slamming into Rahul's chest. The force of the shove sent Rahul tumbling backward.

Rahul's heels scraped against the edge of the container, his arms flailing for balance. He gasped as he felt the world tilt beneath him, and in the next instant, he was falling. His hands shot out instinctively, gripping the cold steel lip of the container just in time.

The world seemed to hold its breath as Rahul dangled over the edge, his feet kicking against the empty air. Below him, the ground stretched far away, the scattered motorcycles and broken crates looking like mere toys from his vantage point.

Karan approached the edge, his face twisted with both triumph and rage. He crouched down, looking over Rahul, his voice a low growl. "You don't know when to quit, do you?"

Rahul's fingers dug into the steel, his knuckles white as he held on for dear life. He glared up at Karan, his jaw tight, his voice steady despite the danger. "I'm not the one hanging on to stolen lives. Let go of this, Karan. It's over."

Karan's expression flickered, a brief shadow of doubt crossing his features, but his sneer quickly returned. "You think you've won? You don't get it, do you? This isn't about motorcycles. This is about power. You'll never take that from me."

Rahul's muscles strained as he pulled himself up an inch, his arms trembling with the effort. "Power? All I see is a desperate man clinging to nothing."

Karan's jaw tightened, his hands balling into fists as he loomed over Rahul.

47

Karan loomed over Rahul, his face twisted in a sinister grin. He raised his foot slowly, savoring the moment, ready to stomp on Rahul's fingers and send him plummeting to the ground below.

"You should've stayed out of this," Karan sneered, his voice dripping with malice.

But before he could strike, a voice rang out.

"Hey!"

Karan froze and turned sharply, his eyes narrowing as he spotted Sanjay standing on the container, breathless but determined. In Sanjay's trembling hands was the prop gun—a remnant of their earlier plans—its barrel pointed directly at Karan.

The sudden arrival and the sight of the weapon threw Karan off. His eyes darted between the gun and Sanjay's face, trying to gauge the threat.

"You think you can scare me with that?" Karan barked, but there was an edge of uncertainty in his voice.

Sanjay's fingers twitched against the trigger. His voice cracked slightly as he shouted, "Move back, or I'll shoot!"

The distraction was a crucial lapse in Karan's focus. In that fleeting moment, Rahul seized his chance. Summoning every ounce of strength, he reached up, his hand locking around Karan's ankle. With a swift, powerful pull, Rahul yanked Karan off balance.

Karan let out a startled cry as his body twisted in the air. He crashed hard onto the steel surface of the container, the impact reverberating like a thunderclap. The prop gun in Sanjay's hands dropped to his side, his shoulders sagging in relief.

Karan groaned, his head spinning from the fall, unable to recover in time. Rahul hauled himself up onto the container, his breaths coming in sharp gasps. He stood over Karan, looking down at the man who had caused so much harm.

Below, the sound of hurried footsteps reached Rahul's ears. He turned to see Inspector Ramana and a team of officers sprinting toward the scene. Ramana's sharp eyes took in the situation immediately. He climbed onto the container with ease, his handcuffs already in hand.

"You're done, Karan," Ramana said firmly, his voice carrying the authority of law. He yanked Karan to his feet, spinning him around before snapping the handcuffs onto his wrists.

Karan struggled weakly, but the fight had gone out of him. "You think this changes anything?" he hissed, glaring at Rahul and Ramana. "There's always someone bigger behind this."

Ramana ignored him, dragging him toward the edge of the container. "We'll see about that."

Rahul straightened, brushing the dirt off his hands. He looked at Karan, then at Ramana. "It's over," Rahul said, his voice low but filled with finality. Satisfaction gleamed in his eyes.

Sanjay, who had been poised to jump into action, relaxed, a smile spreading across his face. He clapped a hand on Rahul's shoulder. "We did it," he said, relief flooding his voice.

Two Days Later

Unfinished Business

The small restaurant was dimly lit, the air thick with tension. Ravi Shetty sat at a corner table, surrounded by a group of rough-looking men. His crisp white kurta was unbuttoned at the collar, his hair disheveled—a stark contrast to his usual composed demeanor. His fist slammed onto the table, the clatter of glasses echoing through the room.

"You idiots ruined everything!" Ravi spat, his voice rising with each word. "One day! Just one day, and it all fell apart. The motorcycles, the operation, my plans—gone!"

The men exchanged uneasy glances but said nothing, their heads slightly bowed as Ravi's rage filled the room.

"You couldn't handle a couple of kids and a crane? What am I even paying you for?" Ravi leaned forward, his sharp eyes scanning the group before landing on a younger man seated at the far end of the table. "And you," Ravi pointed, his voice dripping with contempt. "Why is this gang still called by a dead man's name? Deva's gang. Deva this, Deva that. He's gone. Move on!"

The young man opened his mouth to reply but hesitated, his words dying under Ravi's furious glare.

"Come on!" Ravi roared, slamming the table again. "Answer me! Who's running this circus? Why hold on to a name from the past?"

A low, gravelly voice cut through the tension like a blade.

"Because this empire was built by Deva."

The room fell silent, the weight of those words hanging in the air. All eyes turned to the corner, where an old man sat in the shadows, sipping his tea. He wore a dark leather coat, its edges worn with age, and a beanie pulled low over his head. Round glasses rested on his nose, reflecting the faint glow of the overhead light. Despite the seemingly humble attire, his presence was anything but ordinary. He was built like a mountain, his weathered face etched with lines that spoke of decades of battles won and lost. His presence was quiet but commanding, and when he spoke, it was with the authority of someone who expected to be listened to.

Ravi's eyes narrowed, confusion flashing across his face. "And who the hell are you?" he demanded, his voice sharp but uncertain.

The old man leaned forward slightly, his piercing eyes catching the faint light as he placed the cup down with deliberate care. The silence stretched as he let Ravi's question hang in the air, the tension suffocating.

Then, in a voice that was both calm and chilling, he said, "I'm Deva."

As Deva rose to his feet, his towering presence filled the room. His leather coat shifted with him, the beanie casting a faint shadow over his face while his glasses glinted in the dim light. He glanced at Ravi one last time, his expression unreadable.

"This time," Deva said, his voice like thunder, "I'm taking charge."

With that, he turned and walked out of the restaurant, leaving Ravi and the others in stunned silence. Ravi slumped in his chair, his bravado shattered.

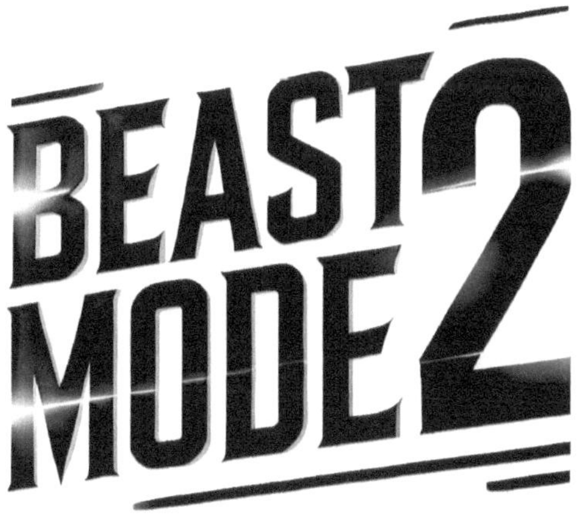

Beast Mode
RELOADED

SOON